SOCIETAL FRAGMENTS

EFFERVESCENT ERRORS

'Debayo Coker

SOCIETAL FRAGMENTS
© Debayo Coker 2014

Published in Nigeria by

Beeni Publishing

381, Borno Way, Yaba, Lagos, Nigeria.
PO Box 3405, Somolu, Lagos, Nigeria.
Tel:+2348033225953/+2349096991619
beeniglobalresources@gmail.com

This is a work of fiction. All of the characters, names, incidents, organizations, and dialogue in this piece are either the products of the author's imagination or are used fictitiously.

ISBN-978-978-941-590-8

DEDICATION

God, the Almighty,
for creating me a survivor.
Inestimable is His kindness to me.

To the memory of my sweet mother,
Esther Omotuyole Coker

And

To every soul that perished with MD-83, Dana Airways Flight on
June 3, 2012.

ACKNOWLEDGEMENT

Christine Wong is a uniquely nice woman who showed me that good people abound still even in the dearth of kindness that pervades the present world. She gifted me a pen whose ink I feel is so priceless. So with that pen I am writing something genuine. She is priceless.

Dianne Hickey is another great person. She read the manuscript in its rough form as we shared ideas and thoughts.

Jeff Underwood and Kate Taylor are two wonderful people; destiny helpers. They took the pains to proofread the manuscript; they shaped and sharpened my writing skills. I am a debutant. I am highly indebted to the both of you.

For every support that I got from many individuals too numerous to mention. I express my gratitude.

My wife, she is pretty, witty, and maturely loving. The perfect woman God created for me.

Societal Fragments

EFFERVESCENT ERRORS

CRIES OF AGONY

MAKING OF A MISANDRIST

PREFACE

Conspicuously and otherwise, our common bond of humanity is, for long, being threatened by humankind itself; as we all are holding sharp knives, somehow, and making attempts to cut that link that bound us; speedily taking us back to Hobbesian man in the state of nature, savagery!

We want transformation but are not ready to change as individuals. Sectionalism, sectarianism, and our inundating quest for materialism, all pervade our sense of attraction.

In one way or the other we are contributory monades to our fortune and fall.

Convincingly, the juxtaposition of the fair quantum of rational beings with a high degree of animosities walking the face of the earth, brings a conclusively dearth of hope for a better tomorrow, but in as much as the rippling pains of disappointments do not start with us, we can stop the continuing reverberation of heartbreaks, if we, in our own little way, will act judiciously.

Respect, appreciation and honor for oneself, for all people, and the entire environment which sustains life are so important in having a peaceful world in all that surround us. Color, gender, age, disability, sexual orientation, education, religion… are not to be considered in doing our bits to making this world of ours to go round.

This is just our minutest fraction we all must contribute to this humanity that we all are part of.

MY FARM! OUR FARM!!

"Cutting these trees
The most enjoyable moments
Of life fulfilling establishments"
The oblivious of next generations
Is totally obvious.
Parading these roads
With great echelons
Around éclat beaming audience
Ovations loud. Standing ones
At every stop over
Smiling coffers
Accruing from every sale of logs.
"As long as I remain the husbandman
To this husbandry
I will fulfill my Machiavellian complex"

"I will cut enough trees
When I gain the affairs of the husbandry
The man there is not getting enough accolades
I will ensure proper disbursement of logs
To the orients and the occident
I will go scouting and hunting for
big log buyers.
Nevertheless,
I will follow the wiseacre:
'Wherever you take care of the sick
You take care of yourself too'
I will add to my retinue
My coffer will know no cry
Family and friends
Beaming with smiles
From Swiss alerts
Hmmm…
For the future
Let's take care of the minute
And am sure the hour will
Care of itself."

"Should I follow the paths

Of my ancestors?
Should I sell the logs
And ensure proper disappearance
Of cowries?
Should I turn the evergreen and the deciduous
Into money spinners
NO!
I will never submit to the
Caprices and malignant
Nature of the past husbandmen
Following the pedigree
Of yester years
Today and tomorrow
I will never prostitute the
Future of children
For a peanut.
I will make a
Revolution
Turning a Manor farm
To Animal farm
Where every animal is equal
Ensuring a proper guidance
Of our collective interest
Accolades today are not the best
On our tombs will be written the history
Of our life
So…
This farm is ours!"

Contents

DEDICATION
SPECIAL THANKS
INTRODUCTION
MY FARM! OUR FARM!!
THE AUTHOR

EFFERVESCENT ERRORS 1

VOICES IN THE
CATHEDRAL...…..……….64

SELF DISCOVERY.. 74

CRIES OF AGONY... 76

JUST ONE MORE... 86

THEY COME AND GO 97

UNFAITHFULNESS...119

IF I SEE..128

A WORLD...……….. 129

MAKING OF A MISANDRIST 134

WOLFSHEEP 151

WONDERS OF MY HEART 158

CINDARELLA 159

PREGNANT WOMAN 162

TO MY HEART... 166

THY HOLINESS... 177

Glossary...179

The Author

'Debayo Coker holds a BA English and Masters in Public and International Affairs from Obafemi Awolowo University, Ile-Ife and University of Lagos, respectively.

An ardent lover of arts and he pursues arts for change. He describes himself as a wordsmith. *Societal Fragments* is his debut. He blogs www.pausibility.wordpress.com

Twitter: adebay_c
debayocoker@gmail.com

SOCIETAL FRAGMENTS

EFFERVESCENT ERRORS

AGEGE. A suburb of Lagos that is inhabited by approximately five hundred thousand people. One of the foremost local government areas in Lagos state, Nigeria, West Africa. It is about thirty minutes drive away from the Murtala Mohammed International Airport (MMIA) on a sane day of traffic in Lagos. Otherwise, productive hours would be rendered useless fighting to rumble through the insanity and nuisance of the usual Lagos traffic. There is an especial knot at the Mongoro junction that links the Lagos-Abeokuta Expressway.

Road rage comes to mind. Blazing sirens that throw one into confusion of which to yield to; the ambulances' or the VIPs'?

One would wonder, even with adequate town planning, whether the menace of this population outburst over the years could adequately have been predetermined. Even the late British Reverend, Thomas Robert Malthus' prediction could not have envisioned that the population would continue to grow and that men would have to learn to survive somehow at the union of a bulge of people and a dearth of infrastructures, combined with a diminishing regard for social amenities.

PEN CINEMA, the heart of Agege municipal district, is always a centre of different activities. Commuters, hawkers, police, shoppers, pedestrian traders, etc. Whatever you look for you will get as hardly would you search before you are pointed in the right direction.

The recent ban of Okada, a form of public transport relied upon by many increased the tempo of activities in and around the arena. Of course, this imposes an abundance of hardship on the people because they rely on this very mode of conveyance. Many children were born believing that motorcycle is a planned urban mass transit mode; to them it is normal. But with their rising popularity, there developed a crazy quilt upon the roadway with these two wheelers weaving in and out of the Lagos traffic. The Lagos State Government banned motorcycles on some roads, this one included. The restrictions and outright ban of the use of the two-wheeled motorized vehicle was predicated on the number of road mishaps they have caused and criminal activities they have been used for too. People now have to wait their turn by queuing up to join the public buses flowing out to their various destinations.

The government is trying her best to bring sanity back into the Lagos clime. The Bus Rapid Transit (BRT) System has been introduced in order to rid the state of the impunity of attitude characterized by the Omni-bus drivers and their system. The BRT buses only ply the dedicated lanes. The hue and cry of any loss by commuters from pick pockets or by any other form of petty pilfering arising from rushing to get on board a bus, is also to be eradicated because each commuter will have to buy himself or herself a bus ticket, take a queue, then board a bus. No rush. Then the criminal loses the advantage of confusion within which to hide.

This approach is typical of what occurred during the Buhari-Idiagbon Military Regime of the early Eighties. That regime termed the programme: War Against Indiscipline (WAI). One would have wondered what it took military officers to teach civilians how to behave civil as people were made to do things with and in a right sense then, but it lapsed as time flowed forward.

The statue of Oba Ogunji adorns the center of the roundabout at Agege Pen Cinema. Some few meters from the statue, southwards, is the railway lane that links Ijoko to Iddo, a connection of two dead ends. The train stations are always filled with people waiting to board to reach their various stops. Early in the morning, many elites, young, vibrant men and ladies are regular callers at the train station. Many of them will be there as early as 5am in order to catch that smooth ride to Iddo Terminus from where they can easily catch a bus to other parts of Lagos Island or Victoria Island as most businesses are situated on the Islands. It is economically sensible for people to live close to their workplace but that is not the case here, as rents on the Island come at skyrocket prices: many buildings there are skyscrapers. Why is it that the taller the building the higher the rent?

A modern day conundrum!

The Island is exquisite for the rich expatriates and high end professionals, as the salary of most workers would not afford them such posh locations. How can a worker who earns less-than-a-dollar-a-day pay the annual rent of about fifteen thousand dollars at the cheapest?

So people prefer to live in the hinterlands and go through the ritual of an early rising and a late return back home, to and from work, each and every day.

The evening traffic craze is indescribable. Hours upon hours are spent on the road, and that amounts to a national loss of vast amounts of productive time. A man who gets home so late at night, manages to eat, jumps into his bed without having time to talk with his family or friends, and jumps up at the beck and early call of his snooze - alarm, his dream within sleep of the good life rudely made to disappear, rushes into the bathroom, hits the road to work at that crack that spells dawn, and comes back home late in the night, repeatedly, *ad nauseum*!

Many cases of death resorting from exhaustion from that kind of strain is a commonplace but a number of people have used the alibi of the traffic to create time for themselves to cheat on their spouses with dalliances on the side. Certain people can be creative with any circumstance. Praise the brain behind the ingenious plan.

"It is this crazy traffic." That is the ready answer to any deviance from punctuality. Of course, it is pardonable because every Lagos resident understands that Lagos traffic is an unpredictable holy terror.

SUNDAY, June 3, Two Thousand and Twelve. A McDonnell Douglas MD-83 with registration number 5N-RAM operated by Dana Airways flying from Nnamdi Azikwe International Airport, Abuja, Nigeria has crashed just a few minutes short of landing at Murtala Mohammed International Airport, Lagos, Nigeria, with one hundred and forty seven passengers and six crew members on board. It crashed into a residential area in Iju-Isaga, West of Oba Ogunji's statue at the roundabout in Pen Cinema, Agege. This news was received by many with sorrow. The Cable News Network (CNN) and other international and local news agencies are zooming in on the story. Nigeria has been in the international news for so many fractured and unworthy reasons lately.

"This is one too many." These statements dropped freely from the lips of people. Truly, many crashes have been witnessed in this year alone.

A great rush towards the crash scene was noticed so swiftly. People from Agege environs and the primary locale of the accident site, all rush to Adeshina Street where the plane was burning and blazing. All roads are blocked within the blink of an eye as many drivers, instead of driving their cars out and away from the scene, all drove towards the scene in order to catch a glimpse of the tragedy.

One would have thought that common sense would have prevailed such that people would clear the paths to the scene for rescue operations and ancillary equipment to reach the site easily and efficiently, especially when there has not been any public training on how to manage a situation of this magnitude. Instead, people trooped out, *en masse*, to witness the scene, gape, and let their cameras rip. Maybe they too can get their bit of film to go viral on YouTube.

Neither illiteracy nor its polar opposite, education, are equipped to dampen the human spirit for gore and others' misery.

Not only were the passengers in the plane victims, but the crash killed many people in the vicinity and as far as the damage can get, with swift flying debris and torn metal. There was also the report of a rescue vehicle running over and killing a surviving passenger: not in this crash though, thankfully. Over thirty people were recorded killed on the ground. A cow was dismembered from the explosion of the crash. As poverty rages in the veins of the young guys there, they started fighting each other over who will get what part of the cow as the fire continued to rage.

Eyewitness accounts stated that the plane burst into flame about twenty minutes after its crash-landed. In a way, if the people that had rushed to the scene had helped, they would have been able to save some lives. But one cannot totally blame the public. This is a climate of colossal bad form where people do not even understand their rights; let alone do they comprehend how to even remotely demand that those rights be enforced. An observation is, that a person who does not have ample opportunities to satisfy fundamental needs, or even a sense of the privilege of casting a ballot, how will such a person be moved to safeguard his life or his neighbors' in times of crises? Education seems to be a guide to better relationships and a greater willingness to aid others; that does put a heavy burden on the significance of education. Possibly, hopefully, there is an instinct to help one another, but not in this case it seems. Before help can arrive, it was already too late.

Both Federal and Lagos State Fire Service, and other agencies like Lagos State Emergency Management Agency (LASEMA), Federal Emergency Management Agency (FEMA), Accident Investigation Bureau (AIB), Julius Berger of Nigeria; a civil construction company, and the list goes on, swung into action. There were so many constraints apart from the huge uncontrollable crowds at the scene. The streets are so narrow that the heavy-duty equipments that were required for such a rescue mission had no easy access to the scene. So, they had to look for alternative routes in order to get to that scene. During all of these maneuverings, passengers and the land victims were sadly dying; they were helpless. Woes are abundant. After much perambulation, the rescue squads arrived, not in the nick of time. People left the scene weeping at the cruelty and disgrace of it all.

The manifest of the travelers showed the names of prominent nationals and non-nationals. The son of a former military Vice President, Chief spokesperson of the national oil company, academicians, professionals, and painfully, includes a family of about six people.

MONDAY, June Four, Two Thousand and Twelve. Fateemah, in the company of her friends, has gone to see the wreckage of the airplane. Burnt corpses were being carried in bags from the scene. Most of the corpses, bagged and not bagged, were unidentifiable. The few recognizable ones were amongst the victims on the ground. A lot of people again trooped out to check the extent of the damage. Property damage was estimated at several millions of naira.

The primal instinct of the living was among the dead and burnt bodies. The wolf is circling its prey even as animal corpses lie within the perimeter. Lives lost were the thing, though. Lives lost so cruelly. God bless the souls of the departed.

Fateemah, in a reflex, returned a wave from a young man. One would have thought they knew one another as she added a doting smile to her waving palm. Her friends continued their walk while she slowed her gait in order for the young man to catch up with her. He indeed followed up the wave with action. They both started smiling at one another instantly, as the young man licked his lips as he planted his eyes on her tantalizing cleavage. She was wearing an undersized black body top with the inscription: *Do Me* and a tight, blue, boy-fitted denim pair of trousers. A brown gladiator sandals adorned her feet. Her breasts were protruding under the body top so that one could easily tell that she was had under covered those boobs with an undersized demi-bra. The two oranges bounced rhythmically to each of her gaits. Her waist chain was showing as the body top left a good view for anyone to see her thong panties as they clasped to her skin far above the top of the boy-fitted denim. You know that kind of view. The kind that might make a Pope rush to purgatory.

"I saw you at the club the other day." The boy's voice led with a casual observation.

"I know; you look familiar."

She is a club-cruiser. Any club in Lagos, name it. She knows it. Especially, when Ikeja is an adjoining neighborhood.

"What are you doing now?" He asked with no iota of committance.

"Where to?" She asked without hesitation in an even bolder style than his.

"My place!". He became as hungry as a wolf now; betraying his libertinage. Immediately, the boy beckoned an Okada and they both mounted the motorcycle. "Oladele!". He called out to the rider, signaling their destination.

Two minutes of fiery speed within a residential area, riding at a speed that reached sixty kilometers per hour was usual. That kept the bystanders wondering, yet not surprised, at the rush typical of an Okada rider, all the more reason why they have been restricted to some areas and never to be seen on the trunk-A roads. They got to destination lickety-split. The miracle was that they arrived alive at all.

The boy quickly handed a hundred naira to the Okada man. He rushed to open the gate. His house was a boy's quarter, a makeshift two bedroom abode with a parlor and its own conveniences. They went in and he slammed the door behind them, his air conditioner was made to come alive just as *Cherry Oh Baby* by UB40 was playing on the stereo. At the same time, he switched on his television set and started showing an adult movie. Within a few minutes the whole room got chilled for the occasion. Life is good. Indeed! Except for the burnt corpses just left behind.

He jumped straight at Fateemah and started fondling her as he rushed to pull off his clothes.

"You did not even offer me anything." Fateemah objected.

"Sorry, I cannot resist these boobies! Don't mind my manners." He then stood up and in few minutes he returned with a cold bottle of Irish Cream liquor drink and two glasses. He poured her some and filled his own glass too. They started to drink.

"Do you know my worth?" she queried.

"Don't worry, I will do you well." He responded exactly to what she asked even though it seemed indirect.

At that instant, Fateemah stood with a zeal to get to the action, the base deal having now been sealed, and asked for a towel. He pointed her towards the bathroom. She strolled into the bathroom seductively in a way telling him to get ready. She closed the door behind her and a few minutes later she came out of the bathroom with the towel covering her from bust to waist, leaving only a view of her sexy long legs.

He was dazed to see a toweled mermaid before him. He rushed at her but she practically kept him at arm's length by stretching her hands out touching him on his chest and pushed him backward slowly as she seductively stroke her upper lip with her tongue. She finally got him to the couch, and like the usual description of a pack of cards, he fell on the sofa weightlessly, leaning himself on it. She stirred provocatively before him, the invitation without doubt. She then let the cover go to reveal the treasure behind the wrapper.

"Hmmm." He moaned his approval.

She put his hands to work, making him stroke her body but with a great restriction regarding her breasts as it is her tradition not to allow anyone to touch them, guarding against her belief that early sagging might occur. He worked his right hand to her backside while the left was used around her lacy catapult-like panties; then he turned her to lay her on the couch while he came astride her on top. He gently kissed her lips as he looked her straight in the eyes. They both curled up to one another. Then he stood up to shift the center table in order to create enough space for their easy movement on the couch and the floor. He moved her to the floor on the well maintained carpet. In a blink, he has her panties removed and her legs spread.

"Hmmm" They both moaned at the same time.

He poured the Irish-cream drink on her well chiseled belly and had his tongue licked the scoop from her navel. She hummed like a guitar chord ready to be plucked a second time. He dropped the bottle gently as he laid beside her and started licking every droplet of the cream with the tip of his tongue all over her body parts. He followed it everywhere, even deep down to hidden regions. He made her groan and she held his head so tightly within her thighs while he concentrated on her Vee. He methodically cleaned up any of the droplets of the cream that were poised there. Her thighs held him vice-like and he felt so happy and heavenly the tighter she squeezed his head – an appreciation of the fine job he was doing, especially as he listened to the accompanying sounds from her. He too was certainly speaking in tongues upon her erotic panorama.   And while so engaged, he drank every bit of her proffered sexual wine.

He traveled inside of her now and they both burst at the same time. DOPAMINE. You know what I mean. And if you don't, it's not hard to figure out.

Just after the crescendo of the action, a knock came at the door. With a glance through the tiny peephole on the door, he saw that his girlfriend had come to call. Unknown to him, she has called his phone often enough to give her some small concern. But, really, how can one hear a phone ring in that kind of situation? With the blast of UB-40 and the porn flick's volume, he was lucky that he heard his paramour's moans. He was truly a man. It is typical of a man to not answer his mother if she comes calling at that moment, especially during the orgasmic combustion. Only a fool answers the door then!

He mentioned to Fateemah that his wife has arrived.

"Your wife?!" She jumped up and started dressing up without cleaning up.

"Forget the story, just clothe yourself." The man was all wolfish fangs now, the job complete, and he was rebuffing Fateemah, throwing her panties to her for her not to forget as she quickly strapped on her bra and top including her denim, all at jet speed; not even the celerity of Jim Carey's *Mask* could move more quickly.

Oh, to have a sheep who complies so easily?

She could have ripped him to shreds for his disturbing impatience with her but she reacted otherwise. She would not want to be a victim of an acid bath. She has been part of a mob that caused grave bodily harm to someone, a friend, via an acid attack. She has given as well as received.

****

Her friends and her, set out on a fateful morning to establish their supremacy in the Aga division of the Iju-Isaga area. It is a street that is notorious for its deeds; similar to Akala street in Mushin and Oju-Ina of Lagos Island. Gangs of boys and girls continuously fight to establish their supremacy. This they do by effecting different vices against anyone perceived to be a rival, just as it occurs in the secret cults in the bowels of the various higher institutions of learning. But here, it is a totally unrefined and a pure survivalists' approach to the street. And can one really use the term "refined" or "unrefined" when it comes to violence in the fight for turf and power and inclusion?

"Sukura, or what is that stupid name of yours?" One of the assaulters said this as she assailed this victim by asphyxiating her.

Sukura belonged to the Pink Brassiere Sisters (PBS) and she was involved with a commercial bus driver boyfriend of one of the friends of Fateemah. They spitefully get involved with one another's boyfriends to show their rivals that they are in control, especially those boys they consider gang leaders. Mostly, many Yellow bus drivers are more powerful at dusk when they cover their faces with night's darkness to show their devilish mastery.

Sukura was badly treated as she was made to kneel down in the center of the street in broad daylight and all sorts of deeds were done to her. She took it in good faith knowing that she will surely stage a reprisal. As they beat her, she looked at them and muttered some inaudible words. Eventually, she was made to go but after a strict warning that she must steer clear of the said boyfriend.

Life continues as everyone maintained their space and stance. Sukura reclined into her shell. Fateemah and her friends continued their 'parole' as the Black Bra Sisters (BBS) that they are.

Exactly, fourteen days after the attack on Sukura, a reprisal came. It was bloody. She organized a strong one. She invited all of her sisters who were bonded in this battle royale. They have all come to avenge an assault on a sister.

Fateemah's friend and her driver boyfriend were relaxing in his shack when they struck. A proper surveillance had been carried out by the ladies. These women, bent on revenge, busted the makeshift door to the room where one of their rival ladies was, hauled her out and bathed her in a liquid substance that was raw acid, through and through. As they carried out the onslaught, the boyfriend retired to his room without interfering or appealing to them to stop.

"Everyman for himself," he said to himself as she screamed his name, for mercy's sake, to come to her rescue. She knew that he could have stopped them if he wanted to. His voice could have halted them. But he wasn't about to lift a finger for her.

Few days later arrests were made. The Black Bra and Pink Bra members altogether were arrested at the behest of the community leader. The victim has become blind with her skin scathingly damaged. She is now forever confined to that state unless she is able to raise huge sums of money so she could be taken to India where a plastic surgeon may have the capacity to correct the deformity. And even then, there would be no assurance that she would ever be able to see clearly again. Her eyeballs were badly impacted by the dangerous liquid. Beauty and hope may have been lost to her for her eternity.

Street warfare is beyond cruel. And actually, beyond stupid too!

Sukura, being a high-profile street girl, made some calls and eventually she and her fellow sisters were released as the Police concluded that she acted in self-defense. A judgment was passed without finding its way before the law court.

The Black Bra Sisters were kept in the cell for another two days but later got released after they were taken, in turn, by the Division Police Officer in charge of the station and his boys on duty. They could only get themselves bailed by getting fresh with the officers.

****

When Fateemah heard that the guy's wife has arrived, she knew better than to ask for a show. Too much bristle can happen over unpredictable things.

After clothing herself, the boy calmed her and told her to act as his long lost sister. As he opened the door, he switched off the adult movies on the screen and reduces the volume of his blasting stereo.

"How are you?" The boy said to his girlfriend, she was never his wife; he isn't married. So why he mentioned her as his wife, even he was uncertain as to that. "I didn't hear you at the door. I don't want my landlord to disturb me which was why I turned the stereo on high volume." Not the most brilliant lie but it passed the test this day. He spoke with much confidence and not at all shaky in his manner. He was the type that a polygraph administrator would find fascinating. He ushered her in, offered her a seat, and before she settled down, he introduced his guest with the smoothness of the inveterate liar. His skills were consummate. "Meet 'em." He pointed at his guest.

Fateemah quickly interjects. "Fateemah, I am Fateemah."

"Yes, Fateemah." He couldn't even remember her name. Sex first, names later, if at all. Some men can sleep with anything. Damn high risk! And what does that say of her low rent offering of herself to him?

The girlfriend grudgingly received Fateemah's outstretched arm. "Nice to meet you." Fateemah jumped up immediately, feeling very ill at ease. She rushed out.

"I will see you some other time." Fateemah hoped not. And the sister excuse was rather sad sack by this point. No sister would truly act this way with her brother and his girlfriend. Would they?

"I will call you." The boy responded in agreement as he walked her to the door and watched her leave.

He was a smart young chap. His classless friends would agree. He engaged in sexual recreation.

The girlfriend is a plus-size lady, a lady of class. They are colleagues from work and both of them were off work for the day as they have synchronized their schedules to enjoy their days off together. She has been without a relationship for a long time as many men like their lady slim or moderately built. But, she is the voluptuous type that, if a man falls on her, she will cushion the man so well from being injured. At a point, she had tried dieting but had to stop; she was cautioned by a doctor after she nearly passed out due to a stomach ulcer she sustained following a slim-quick-fix diet. She tried for months and nothing was lost, not even a noticeable pound of fat. Then, she submitted her weight to fate believing that her own man would come into her life regardless of her size.

Facticity, people should not be judged by their build. There have been actual cases where the slim figured ladies lose their men to the plus size ladies. It is one thing to be beautiful, another to have a good heart and a good head.

A toothpick stands nary a chance against an outsized heart.

When he finally asked her out she was so happy; she has been without a relationship for years and will surely not want to be missing the good touch of a capable man like himself. He came with that genuine ulterior motive. She predictably jumped at his request and started sleeping with him even before the end of their first date.

Could it be that she has truly missed the touch of a man? Was it that she felt that she could only keep him with sex? Or was she doing it without minding pregnancies' possibilities whether he accepts the responsibility or not? Many questions!

Immediately after he watched Fateemah leave, he pounced on his girlfriend who never bothered to probe further who the guest was, or their relationship.

Fateemah need not have worried a show whatsoever as his girlfriend was not of that breed. He started tickling her below her ribs and she smilingly delivered herself into his arms. No real issue, or communication goes on between them, whenever they meet, it is for sex. Anyway, his primary reason for wooing her is to have her at his beck and call, for the all-in-all of sex, nothing more, nothing less. But as time goes by, he found her to be useful, as she would cater to him by cooking his meals, doing his laundry, and other household chores, never asking for money and always ready to satisfy him in and out of bed. The kind of woman who will pay you to marry them, beg you to impregnate them, take care of the baby, and possibly other women you may bring in afterwards.

One cannot explain their sense of kindness or gullibility; or the man's willingness to take advantage of it.

****

The government needs to have a mental evaluation for its drivers. And the laws of the road must penalize the government bus driver equal to penalties meted out to any defaulting driver, commercial or private. Otherwise, how can one explain someone who totally ignores the traffic rules and drives against the good of the trafficking public? Definitely, there must be some encouragement of good reasoning so that the driver, the passenger, and the public at large are not threatened by lunatics behind the wheels of large and intimidating vehicles.

In the face of the menace of chronic traffic jams that are synonymous with Lagos, the government has been making moves by the establishment of a traffic management body to work alongside the federal authorities.

The Lagos State Traffic Management Authority (LASTMA) was created to work with the Federal Road Safety Commission (FRSC) and Kick Against Indiscipline (KAI) to maintain sound discipline amongst the populace; part of which is to arrest pedestrians who, in the face of apparent dangers of crossing the busy expressway, despite the availability of pedestrian bridges that have been built by the government, chose the path of danger, where many have been killed or maimed.

Woe betide the world of crazy drivers and crazy pedestrians. Lagos has a full set of both!

All the gathered officials, LASTMA, FRSC, and KAI, will also work with the police. The synergies coalesce and are taking on the task enthusiastically even in the face of the ever-present politics and corruption.

Not too long separated from the establishment of these regulatory agencies, after months of recorded successes and some sanity on Lagos roads, much of the populace relapsed into chaos. The marshals that were employed, most of who were unrehab 'area' boys and girls, poorly trained, soon became corrupt as their priors. People learned how to quickly and readily pay their way through anything, anytime. A minimum fine of twenty five thousand naira was included in the penalties for traffic violations and most people learned that if about ten naira was offered a traffic marshal for his own keep, instead of paying the full twenty five thousand naira into government coffers, the marshal would collect it; readily, happily. It is a government that no one trusts anyhow. Most marshals even become willing to be the ones to haggle for larger bribes.

This is done and a free society is still expected. Did I mention the Vehicle Inspection Unit (VIU), formerly Vehicle Inspection Office (VIO), as one of the agencies that sanitizes our roads?

Every agency is identified by its own uniform. The LASTMA officials wear a butter-yellow shirt and burgundy pair of trousers, the FRSC marshals wear a carton color shirt on a black pair of trousers, the KAI marshals wear a lemon color shirt on a moss green pair of trousers, and the VIU guys wear a white shirt on a black pair of trousers. Needless to say, their uniforms are dressed with many pockets and usually they are put to good use as most of them go back home with pocketful of money, raked in from commuters and traffic defaulters.

"I have an official daily target." One of the marshals answered when asked why he was akin to a merciless wolf in executing his duties. He concluded with, "And I have to take money home."

People are not surprised to hear that invocation as it is a norm in the paramilitary, police and with many agencies in the land.

Many wondered many times, which office? To this question there is no answer. On many occasions, the heads of those agencies, including the police force, come out to deny such allegations. But not long before they stride down the podium, their boys are back on the streets to set up roadblocks purposely to scratch more money out of the commuters or passersby. Anyone who refuses to pay these dues will have to face some bigger punishment. Hence, the fear of these agencies is understandable.

****

The boy saw his girlfriend off to the bus stop so that she could run her errands. They rode on a bike together to the bus stop.

"Easy!" That was the instruction he gave the rider as he sped recklessly down the road, negotiating bends without caution. They almost collide with an oncoming vehicle that was finishing its own bend of the crescent they rode through. The biker has given the third finger salute to the driver of the vehicle and then moved on without stopping to look back.

As his girlfriend mounted the front cabin on the omni-bus taking her seat beside the driver, he muttered to the bus driver, "that is my queen" and also signaled him thumb up. The thumb up signal was meant for the driver to ride gently. Social discourse at play.

It was not rush hour yet so the calmness on the road was sensed and appreciated. The driver signaled back to acknowledge his recognition. The bus sped off. But smoothly if not slowly.

He decided to trek home home in a bid to catch up with a lady who alighted from the same bus that his girlfriend just boarded.

Soldier–go-soldier-come approach.

He walked behind the lady for a while before he decided to accost her. You know when a man clears his throat in anticipation of talking to a new catch. He thinks of himself as a cute guy, about five feet six inches in height, not rotund, and despite his many sexual escapades; he has much vim and vigor in him.

"May I help with your load?" He offered to help as he ran from behind her to lift the sack she was carrying on her left arm as she also struggled with her big handbag that was hanging on her right shoulder. He took the load from her without offering her the chance to respond. He smiled as he took hold. The lady smiled back.

Somewhere else, he would have gotten the flat of the purse against his head for such antics.

"Where are you going?"

"Oladele." The lady replied.

With a leap of joy in his heart, "what a coincidence!" he responded.

How does one live with oneself, possessing such a smug and sleazy mixture of characteristics? He does have much growth potential though.

He stopped a commercial bike with much zest, mounted the bike and asked the lady to mount in behind him. That is, for them to share the same bike. But the lady blatantly objected. She stopped another bike and they rode separately but on the same route to Oladele.

Well, at least she has a scrap of sense.

He asked his biker to slow down and take a cue from the other bike as he did not know the number of the house where the lady was heading. To his amazement, the lady's bike stopped right in front of his gate, his house. He followed the lady as she opened the gate and went in. He was more surprised as his landlord's children ran to greet the lady and helped her with her bag, but instead she beckoned them to him so that they could take the sack from him. She is his landlord's niece, unbeknownst to him.

****

He chose to live in Iju-Isaga because the contractors he was working for have just been commissioned to manage the Iju Water Works; one of the biggest in the state, that was built by the Israelis during the colonial period. He was a Quality Control expert, having studied Biochemistry in the university. He has a good brain and he graduated top of his class. He has been working with the Chinese for about seven years now and he was appointed to lead the Quality Control team in the Iju Water Works.

His landlord looked at him with a warning sign that indicates: steer clear. He knew his bubble has been popped on this one.

Fateemah has kept a lookout somewhere close to the house so she will get her money. She can't render such a service for free, though she enjoyed the guy so well. This guy performed well for her, she climaxed righteously, but she was not fully satisfied yet. He owed her still. Business is business and should be kept at that, especially when there is a clause of contract that is binding though unwritten.

As he laid deflated on his couch, she banged on his door and he looked through the peephole as usual and his spirit came back to life seeing that there is bound to be another pleasure ride.

"Did you see that a lady just went in? He changes them as quickly as a chameleon easily grafts onto the color of its environment."

The landlord has retired from teaching after putting in the statutory number of years. He knew all about the going-in-and-out of the boy and his many guests, mostly girls. He loaded his niece's ears with what his eyes have seen when she enquires about the guy downstairs. The landlord was out to protect his niece from the dude.

"I have seen him with more than twenty girls since he began living here." Then he spat into the sink.

The niece is a Registered Nurse who was working at one of the prestigious health institutions in Lagos. She just visited the village and has some messages for the landlord which necessitated her visit to his house on that day. The sack she had with her contains some foodstuffs. Abundant fresh food stuffs are found in the villages and most of them perish due to lack of proper warehousing system as well as good roadways to transport them to the cities where the best markets exist. The few that are able to make it to the cities are so highly priced; a sad mechanism of supply and demand.

She got turned off by all that she heard from her uncle but there was a tinge of his kindness that remained with her.

"All the same, he is a nice man." She said this quietly so that her uncle cannot hear.

One note here. Were there any women who understood the word "gullible"? Intellectually, maybe. Emotionally, hardly. What if she is correct though?

By the time Fateemah stepped out of his room, his portion of the contract was fulfilled. He has both satisfied her again and fulfilled her needs, such that both parties smiled upon its completion. Now the contract has been fully considered; signed, sealed, and delivered. There was a fiscal responsibility on his part and a sexual satisfaction provision on her end. There was now no need for a third party intervention. Defaulting on this kind of deal is an infraction.

Just as he opened the gate for Fateemah to go out of the house, the lady upstairs came down about the same time preparing to leave.

Courteously, he held the gate for the lady to pass just after Fateemah has departed. He bade her goodbye but instead she stretched her arm for a handshake. As he held it, a sharp feeling rushed down his spine. Her palm was succulent and the warm handshake showed a good ease of friendliness. Her brilliant smiles and bright eyes were overlaid by chromic lenses held in a designer frame. She has some kind of ingrained confidence. Not to argue that she is a matured lady, though her petite figure did not betray much. She smelled good.

She softly jerked him back to life as she read that he was somewhat lost in his imagination. He returned her smile as he held onto to her arm still.

The landlord watched from the balcony of his apartment that was adjoining the rear of the compound as they both exchanged numbers. She was his matured niece who was in her late-thirties. She could not be said to be making a mistake at her age and with her experience and exposure. She has survived quite a number of thunderstorms. She climbed on a waiting bike to take her to her connecting bus stop.

****

The flexibility of his work schedule allowed him the luxury of time. He worked four days per week. This was very rare with a Chinese business. Typically, they work people to the bone, especially when they know that the unemployment rate is so high and people are willing to do anything to gain and stay in employment in order to earn a living wage, even less than a living wage often.

This should not be the case in a land that is vastly blessed with many mineral resources but lacking righteous leadership to harness the wealth for the country's advancement and general benefit of the population. Wealth in the ground goes nowhere. What is brought up from the ground's core, oil mainly, is either owned by international companies, is siphoned off by native sons who fill their own pockets, or is shut down by rebels and terrorists attempting to divert some of the yellow gold emerging from the black kind into their own coffers. And the law be damned from one and all groups. For the patsy, the common laborer, there is no regard for human dignity as the machinery operates without the installation even of the necessary safety equipment as enshrined in the Safety, Health and Environment (SHE) guide under the Labor Act. The government has conducted many inquests into recorded accidents in such companies but nothing concrete has ever been resolved.

When justice is put up for sale, there is no complainant or accused; but the highest bidder gets what it grabs.

NIGHTTIME, Aga would come alive with activity. The boys would have come back to their base after a hard day's drive round the city. The day is just starting. The girls would take a fresh bath; cologne; make up; and a gorgeous dress. And for the boys, a cool bath and a new dressing, most of them decked their black finery on a black night. Everyone in different clusters and hordes. Each man and woman sidles up to his and her group. A street show-off must be done to know who just bought what new thing. It's the proverbial peacock strut. This after hours of perambulation continues until almost midnight. The boys would retire to the base, armed, and then hit the town. The girls would call on their cab drivers and hit the clubs; mostly clubs in Ikeja. Ikeja is known as the heart of entertainment on the mainland. They would stand on the roadbeds, dressed scantily, displaying their wares just like any other market. They would be picked, sometimes taken to hotels or homes for a short time or for a Till-Day-Break (TDB) treat, depending on the bargain.

The nature of the activity smacks of john and ho but no one likes to think in those terms. It is a bit too honest for those who hate to prick their self-inflated egos.

TUESDAY. June Five, Two Thousand and Twelve. They returned home in the early hours of the morning. The boys and their loots. The girls and their exploits. There is usually a sync sometimes where the girls enlist the service of the boys in order to deal with a client who they perceive to be rich-but-tight-fisted or who has not treated them fairly. The boys go deal with the client in their way, a bit of thuggery is usually involved, and successfully retrieve the loots so that all contracts are fairly and wisely met. Promiscuity has its own price and any man that is foolishly ready to ignore the warning of its risks, usually ends up being a loser every which way. Fateemah has been a snitch to the boys and to the police on many an occasion. A cockroach is told to go infest some food and then a fowl is set after it.

They would go to bed when others were waking and getting ready for work. They would sleep till about midday. Then the boys would go out after midday and drive the commercial buses till late in the evening and the girls would go out to do afternoon hustle depending on availability.

Adeshina Street witnessed a lot of activities as so many government dignitaries and politicians made it a sudden Mecca of sorts. They had come to make political statements. How gory this is? A politician standing on a crash site giving speeches about the departed when he should have acted to prevent the incident, by putting the right measures in place so that such occurrences are minimized while ensuring that the emergency response is quicker and adequate. The pretty picture breaks down, the ugly one stands close to it.

The State Governor had come the previous day and the President flew into Lagos from Abuja, the seat of power, the following day. He joined a convoy from the airport to Adeshina. All roads were cleared with policemen lacing the street beds all the way from the airport to the crash scene; as if to compass the President to the destination. The usual no-landing signal had been given to all craft in the sky to go elsewhere or continue hovering in the sky for as long as their jet fuel will last and for as long as the President will be flying or landing. Also, whenever the President is coming to town all roads are closed till he departs. It is a major inconvenience to the people.

Each time he came to town, it was one hell of a day that productive time will be wasted on the road because his entourage would trample on people without reason. Long traffic jams that would last hours to clear, will be recorded resulting into chaos and crises on the road. His coming should be a blessing such that his boys would have helped in clearing any gridlock that people may have been experiencing on the road before his arrival; but far from it, they created mayhem , more mayhem than they met.

An unprecedented pressure was put on Adeshina Street from the rush of humans to have a view of the President.

The rescue operation will have to be brought to an end in a few days.

****

The boy had called the landlord's niece. She returned his call because she was not available when his call came. She was attending to a patient at that time.

"I saw a missed call from you."

"I am sorry if I disturbed you." He was being a gentleman. Ordinarily, he would not call a lady just to check on her without wanting them to come over.

"It is no problem. Thank you for checking on me." The call ended. She was softening.

He fantasized how sweet it would be to hold her in his arms. To talk with her again. To smell her neck. She got ingrained in his thoughts for the rest of the day.

Fateemah had gotten a hint from one of the boys about a bloodbath that may go down so she called her newest client to know if he would be available in a bid to avoid the fracas that would break out any time in the area. He told her he would return her call to let her know when he can be available as he did not see any need to tell her that he was at work. They were not on dating terms, after all. More so, his regular girlfriend will be home with him to observe their ritual daily sextivity. He had thought the plus-size was attempting to lose weight by working out through sex; a Pauline Potter style and wouldn't want to break her routine, especially when it was at no cost to him.

****

That afternoon, the different, rival confraternity groups of the boys gathered all their available weapons. New faces infiltrated the area; mercenaries, in anticipation of a big fight. Pay them and they will fight on that side. Just like the Middle

Ages. Conscripts, mercenaries, call them what you will. It has been a while since the area experienced such a big fight. The last time was when a battle was waged to ascertain the sexuality of one of the boys that belong to Eiye Confraternity.

The boy was being wooed by the core male homosexual confraternity for they saw him living their world. His effeminacy was mistaken for homosexuality; stereotypes seen as reality. It happens all of the time. It was a battle that lingered on the lips of so many that the police at the Red House Police station could not contain it until the officers of OP-MESA; a joint patrol of the police and the military, a security machinery organized by the state government to quell rising criminal activities in the state, were drafted in.

Effeminacy is mostly mistaken for homosexuality. It is a perception that many people have of a man that suggests one thing or the other which gives him an affectation that might make him look like the female gender. At its most superficial, it is just the physical approach which gets stereotyped. A man that pierces his ears may be cast out to be a gay in some quarters.

Femininity, on the other hand, core womanliness, is determined by environment and genes. It is sometimes problematic as a transgender person will tell you. But, if a man exhibits certain deeper traits openly, traits considered exclusively attributable to a woman, or a man who is sexually attracted to men only, then the label of gay is applied by those who are gay and other than gay. A man who believes that he is a woman trapped within the body of a man is a more complex dynamic. That's a story for another day; it's truly beyond the scope here. It is a field that maintains dynamic ebb and flow of discourse which is still far from finished. Many see it as simple and they label with the ease of the ignorant.

Feminism, on a general note, is associated with ensuring the proper treatment of women, by and from women and men. But in this clime, not so many people have or subscribe to this particular view; men and women alike. Feminism has not echoed through the halls here as it has elsewhere. One might wonder why that is? Possibly were feminism taken to the breast by the people, the events about to occur would grow less and less. Feminism confers dignity on a woman. A woman of dignity rarely street-fights nor does anything unladylike.

In such a street fight, bottles, axes, cudgels, and sometimes, guns are freely used. At times, the battle rages on for days, depending on the response of the security operatives at the Police Station in that area. If it is too small and not adequately equipped to contain the audacity of those miscreants, damage becomes multifold. There have been cases where the officers that were to execute the law found enjoyment in the rollercoaster ride alongside these boys as some of the officers would be bought over so cheaply with a bottle of gin and other tiny gifts. The moral right to condemn and arrest any form of nefariousness is lost when the executor is himself a beneficiary of the largesse from that crime. Most officers, world over, are stereotyped as very willing to partake of the forbidden fruit.

Everyone got the signal and scampered for safety as soon as the first bottle was smashed on the ground. On a day like that, the girls, those who have afternoon jobs, always count themselves lucky as they would take refuge wherever they are. Sometimes, they even go with men for free for days, so long as the fight lasts, just to enjoy the refuge away from the fight.

Aga is that façade that would greet you with serenity upon arrival. The calmness of the pose camouflages the totally taut energy about to uncoil. It is about to erupt in one of the worst and least managed settlements. The narrow road leading into the big community is directly opposite the Elliot bus stop along Iju-Ajuwon road, just a minute away to Grail Land, the national headquarters of The Cross Bearers.

****

The boy went home earlier than usual today without having to wait for his office paramour to go home with him as customary. She was not happy that he left the office without letting her know, but she will never show it. She never complained about anything he did and that was already turning him off.

He submitted, when jokingly asked by his landlord the kind of lady he would like to have for a wife, "someone cerebrally engaging, responsible, goodly, even Godly, hygienically careful, organized, and with an expressionistic beauty", such words without even thinking about it, really.

The landlord was bewildered by these particular set of adjectives he posited. He expected that he would have mentioned some physical qualities. But that was not even intended in his submission. Though the landlord hasn't interacted with all the girls he has seen with him, yet none that he has engaged in conversation has any one of these qualities at her core. His colleague from the office was gentle but not convincingly cerebral.

He reread the text message he sent, about midday, to the landlord's niece: *I live my story via the apparent conviviality of my expression. I hope that your day is going well?*

Spoken or written, he has a way with words when it comes to women, which make them look forward to meeting him again and again, but this time the lady nurse did not respond expressly as he waited for her response.

A knock on his door punctured his imagination. He opened the door for his colleague but he was not in the mood for sex this time which got the colleague wondering. He did not grab her as usual. They both mutely sat and watched the television and as soon as there was blackout, from the power grid operated by the Power Holding Company of Nigeria (PHCN), he got an ample alibi to leave the house and asked that she lock the door when she would be leaving. She felt dejected as he has never treated her this way, before. Ordinarily, he would have gone to switch on the generator and then have her sexually ruffled up but it was a different scenario tonight.

"Maybe something is eating him up, better still, he is tired of me.", she said, but she wasn't upset as expected in a normal dating relationship. She left to her home.

WEDNESDAY, June Six, Two Thousand and Twelve. Another early morning rise to work. He preferred trekking to work than to drive his Sport Utility Vehicle (SUV), a tool- of- trade given him as a work vehicle. He saw that as a form of another physical exercise apart from his sexual exertion. A safe variation from his usually sedentary at work. He would sit in his fully air-conditioned office doctoring the requisition for the job done, even though he was supposed to be overseeing the technicians as they chlorinate the water before the public consumption. He saw no need for that for he believed that they have learnt enough on the job to be certified experts. He perfected the data for each day and in turn he compromised the stock through the chemical supplier. He was the QC lead, thus he has influence on who supplies what, such that his favor was usually curried by the suppliers. He considered his a lesser crime to unbridled stealing being carried out by the political elites.

He got accosted on the road by a police officer who demanded that he identify himself. He felt so maligned by that request because he recently read how the police illegally arrest and detain people and in the end demand money to be paid for bail even though it is publicized that: BAIL IS FREE.

"Who are you?" the officer asked rudely. So typical.

He stood still and asked the officer, "What do you mean?"

"*Adentify yasef!*" He shouted with the common accent.

He felt violated by such a rash treat and he refused to bring out his Identity card. As a Nigerian, he has every right to move freely, anywhere or anytime in any part of the country without the fear of molestation or attack. And what does showing an ID card change if criminals can carry phony ID cards of blue chips with inscriptions of juicy positions as their occupation? The real criminals don't advertise their identity publicly and the police dear not wait to have a second view of the ID cards.

"What if I don't have an ID card?" He queried back.

"*I will have to arrest you be dat.*" The police officer responded in uncouth fashion.

"What if I am jobless or an artisan, better still, I have left my ID card somewhere?" He was ready to probe and test his limits.

"The way you dress, you no fit be an artisan." A profiling of some sort?

His countenance changed as it is ridiculous for someone to be arrested for not being able to present an ID card. He raised his voice and started expressing the bitterness he has bottled up against the some nefarious activities carried out by the police. Many people would want to do same, but he has the audacity to express his views where others would not. He was just being bold as he has chosen to live his life minus fear or intimidation from anybody. After all, since the constitution, even though its currency is weak in the present social and political climate of the day, guarantees such rights. He was determined to do anything possible to exercise those constitutional rights of his.

The tension started to build up at the intersection leading to his office and the most senior officer on that patrol came closer. He continued to grouse and angrily brought out his official ID card, showed it to the officers and told them that he was not one of those whom they could cheaply harassed as he pointed to a busload of arrested people. He further harassesed them with regards to the unlawful detention simply because ID Cards cannot be presented.

Many people were not covered in the last National ID card scheme which was marred by a lot of unsavory practices. And what if they had even misplaced their ID cards? There was no way they could get them replaced as such a provision was not at all a part of the program. It is sheer injustice! The distasteful thing about the arrest was that these people will be taken to a corner side, ransacked, and then made to cough up some amount of money as bail; anyone who could not pay the bail amount, will of course, have to be detained and slammed with grievous offences that could mar his or her destiny. A lot of people in these police cells are languishing there because they have not been able to meet the monetary request for their bail by the police. Prisons are also congested on the account of unnecessary delay in the justice system.

The senior officer calmed him down courteously and explained that theirs was a crack team that was just carrying out lawful checks and most times, the arrests helped in foiling so many robberies. He accepted his explanation understandably because of his civil approach to the issues, unlike his subordinates who were reeking of alcohol in the very early hour of the morning while on duty. He was apologized to and left to go.

He headed for his office as that was his wont anyway, hand-in-pocket. As he took his seat, he beheld a card on his desk with a note: I am sorry if I did anything wrong.

Most women think once a man does not talk to them for a moment, it has to do with an offense they have committed or that he does not like them anymore, or that he is seeing someone else. Flippant excuses start to flow.

He crushed the note and dropped the card in his drawer as he was still pissed from the police harassment. He felt sorry for those that were arrested. He softened up as he read the SMS from the nurse: Thank you! My day went well. I hope you are good?

She was busy all through yesterday. That was the reason for her delayed response, but better late than never. It came eventually.

She was living her passion as she has a good caring heart and she has chosen her career path so perfectly. She attended the prestigious Queens College, Lagos for her secondary school and the University of Ibadan for her university education where she studied Nursing and Midwifery. Always she put everything humanly and positively possible to ensure that she reached the zenith of her career in her chosen profession. Above all, her happiness of affecting lives positively by providing adequate medical care for the sick and disabled could not be mouthed. Many times, she has had to choose between her relationship and her passion. Each time, she chose the latter because she believed that any man that will marry her will have to understand and accept that passion. Her relationships usually hit the rocks on complaints that she barely had time to spend with her partner. She would make them understand the nature of her work and how much fulfillment she derived from her career path but most of the men are traditionalists that would want her to do some household chores as well as warm their beds. To the latter, she has little objection but not usually available to attend to some chores. She was almost married six years ago but the suitor's family convinced him otherwise on the grounds that nurses are usually flirtatious. And the 'boyman' unwisely listened to and acted on their ignorance.

Maturity is being responsible for your decisions and living with them, good or bad, but not all men have those traits. They allow friends, family, and some other insignificants decide for them. Anyway, his loss, and she moved on.

She had few relationships since. And sometimes her culture has made her feel that she was in the twilight of her beauty and doomed to a single life. Cultural enlightenment is not always so. Cultural expectations devastate so many lives unnecessarily.

He left the office at midday, drove to the Island and sat on the beach. The drive was smooth because, during that time, the harshness of the road was usually dampened and in about forty five minutes he got to the Bar Beach. As he was enjoying the calm ambience, he decided to call the nurse. Her phone hardly rang this time before she picked it up and she agreed to come meet him by the beach. She had come from a nearby office on her two hour break.

"Do you come here often?" She asked that as they settled in to chat.

"Not really. Only when I am stressed." He responded.

"What is itching that brought you here today then?"

He narrated his ordeal while on his way to work and how sorry he felt for those guys who were arrested. He felt helpless that he could not aid them.

"There is nothing much we can do at this time but be steady and stalwart. We all do what we must do to change the situations that we don't like. Our cumulative efforts will yield expected results and we will live as the good human beings that we are, somehow, someday." He looked deep into her eyes as she rolled out those words. Her words prove to be consoling. She was youthfully dressed in a tailored red shirt on a smartly sewn, lively cream colored set of boot cut chino pair of trousers. They smiled as they ate their order of, ketchup covered, spiced fries and bacon.

"Too much of these are not good after all". She ate them with a slightly jaundiced eye.

"I don't have a pot; bachelor that I am." He was discreetly alerting her to his availability. She feigned ignorance. "I thought that you live at my uncle's with your wife?" A bit of counter probing on her part. The dance began. "No, I am not married." He simply stated.

"I thought the lady that you opened the gate for the other day was your wife." She pressed him and that was good. She was interested.

"She is just a friend." He gave one of those pregnant smiles.

She looked at her wristwatch and then, rose to leave. Back to work. The two hours have flown by as they enjoyed each other's company very much.

"Hope there is no problem?"

"I am an employee." Jokingly, she told him that she needed to go back to work because her break was over. He offered her a ride back to her office but she refused politely, giving the excuse that she needed to get something along the way for her colleague. He wisely did not push too much but walked her to a cab. The Red Cab is one of the rare positive initiatives where the Lagos State Government is elevating the transportation system to meet the standards of other cosmopolitan areas; like New York, Tokyo or Berlin. More power to Lagos! He loved to let his mind meander into social and political observations that affect all. He bade her farewell and hinted that he would be very happy if they could do this again some other time.

As he went back to catch a bit more of the cool breeze, he saw Fateemah and her friends seated in front of one of the shacks used as shelter by prostitutes on Kuramo Beach. They have bailed from the Aga area for quite some days now, waiting for all of the tensions to douse. The shack owners, mostly miscreants, who have turned the beach side into a home, charged a stipulated amount for the prostitutes to practice their trade. Some ladies operating in that particular red-light district don't use the shacks and they perform outside on the beach sand at the strip's far end. They would not usually charge for any accommodation as it is a very quickie thing. Those who use a shack must surcharge their clients. The fee must ultimately go to the landlord, the shack owners.

She came over as he beckoned her, sat next to him, smiled and asked, "*you dey come here too?*"

"*Dis na my area.*" He responded in the usual we-rock-this-town attitude.

He probed to know what her mission was by the beach at this time of the day. He once thought that she was a medium level prosty, not just a cheap whore. What difference does it make really though? High-profile, mid-profile or low-profile. As soon as a woman charges for sex, she has decently descended into the abyss of moral and social decadence. So too the pimps and johns as well. Freely are ye given. He recollected his fling with this woman.

Fateemah is a Nigerien who has fled her home country, Niger, in a bid to escape being married off to an older man at a tender age. She came to Nigeria through the North-East border of the country. She had witnessed many of her friends married off at ages of between nine and thirteen to men old enough to be their fathers and grandfathers. Many of them ended up as one of the many wives of the man. Eventually they suffered Vesico-vaginal Fistula (VVF) and Recto-vaginal Fistula(RVF) disorders. Both fistulas are caused as a result of pressure exerted by the fetal head on the somewhat immature pelvis during a difficult labor; a force that interrupts the blood flow to the nearby tissues in the mother's pelvis.

VVF occurs when the blood supply to the tissues of the vagina and bladder is restricted during a prolonged and agonizing labor. The tissues between these organs die, forming holes through which urine passes uncontrollably. RVF on the other hand is caused in the same fashion but this damage is done between the tissues of the vagina and the rectum, leading to an uncontrollable leakage of feces. These two are prevalent risks associated with child marriage.

As decadent as the practice of child marriage is, some people, politicians, religious leaders, fully support it, and are even ready to fight and argue in its favor on the floor of the legislative houses so that it can be legalized. How much some men, depraved as they are, would shamelessly and publicly exert their perversion and power? The law that is to bind, is blind to its own atrocities at the push of the benighted, though cognizant enough to know that it is repulsive and wrong actually.

Fateemah thought that she had escaped from the devil, hoping to find a better life in the country she has crossed into, but little did she know that she has to face greater devils. First, she had to convince the authorities that she was not one of the insurgents that the government is fighting with. Once that hurdle had been crossed, she was faced with sexual molestation by multiple men. Her first night in Chibok, after a long tiring drive through the desert in the back of the truck that brought her and her compatriots in fear into Nigeria, was harrowing. She laid on a bench in the park because they arrived in the dead of the night. A certain man that traveled with them offered her a sachet of water, he knew that she would be so thirsty after the long desert travel. She jumped from the bench, took the water with much happiness, and gulped it down. From that simple action, a feeling of "victory at last" enveloped her. The man sat close to her on the bench and put his hand around her neck and muttered some words that she could only interpret to be the descendance of danger.

She woke up to find herself being stared at by bystanders in the park; clothes shredded such that one could take her for a deranged person; semen and blood were all over her. She had been raped. By how many men, she could not tell but with the activities around her she could tell it was not just one man. That was her gory initiation into sex at age twelve. The evil that she dreaded most had happened to her. Bad enough, the money she stole from her father to facilitate the trip had also been stolen. Some good Samaritans showed concern by providing her a new set of clothing and feed but for that gesture only lasted two days. She had to survive somehow and she resorted to alms begging, a common practice in that part of the country.

Many children of school age are out of school following in the nomadic steps of their ancestors. A great number of such definitely contribute to the data of the millions of children the United Nations submitted to be out-of-school in Nigeria. A great worry because a nation that cannot educate her youth is sitting on a keg of gunpowder that will inadvertently lead to her destruction. Even though they have eyes they will live in perpetual blindness. Such are easy recruits for devilish orchestration.

She hustled for her survival and sometimes gave in to sex with the nomadic boys in exchange for *fura* - cow milk - and food.

With her amiable personality, one of the women took an interest in her and promised to ground her in a business. As time went by, she mastered a trade during the day but at night engaged in the oldest trade of all times. She would have to cede sixty percent of her earnings to the Madame and naively she agreed. The woman provided her shelter, clothing, and food. In the night they went out together. Because she was a new face in the business and considering her young age, as some men prefer them even younger than their own daughters, she received great patronage and true to the agreement, she ceded the agreed upon percentage to the woman. Ten months into the business, she was able to establish a solid enough foundation to be able to get a place of her own. She decided it was high time to renegotiate her agreement with the woman. She approached her with a twenty percent offer but the woman rejected it altogether, Fateemah balked, her patroness became angry and threatened her; telling her that she was bound by the agreement for as long as she would remain in that business in that town. Fateemah was not bothered by this as she now knew her way around the town well enough. She had some of the officials of the Joint Task Force (JTF), the joint patrol team of the armed forces and the police, set up to fight the Boko Haram scourge ravaging the Northeast, as clients, so she was not moved one bit.

A few months after her independence from the woman had been established, many customers still lining up at her doorstep on a regular basis. Her trade was booming as clients passed to one another the service of a thirteen year old girl. Referrals just flew her way. Tragedy struck soon enough. An elderly man had come to have a taste of her pot. And after many rounds of hot sex, the aged man slumped. She shouted for help as it was horrific for her. She had never witnessed anyone dead before, let alone someone dying on top of her while still inside of her. The old man was rushed to a nearby clinic and was certified dead. She was almost mobbed, but the intervention of the JTF officers rescued her from the crowd and they handed her over to the police at the station. She was detained for days and released a week after, but only after the cause of death was certified to be not of her making but, according to the medical team's findings. The old man died from exhaustion involving his inability to survive marathon sex. However, she still was made to bail herself out. She pleaded that she should be given a rebate and with a promise of free service for some weeks, as the officer that was in charge of the case was one of her clients, she was followed home to get the bail bond, after which, she struck one day off her weeks of sexbiz to the officer. She freshened up and had a good rest in preparation for the business at night. This tragedy was not so overwhelming as to keep her from a positive return to her business.

That night, while inside the room with a client, she heard shouts of shock and fear from people trapped in an inferno that was already raging through the shacks lined up at the village end. She and everyone else scampered for safety. She and her client jumped out, almost naked. Everything was crisped. All her life's savings that she kept in a container too. Everything. Not a needle was spared.

That was her true tragedy!

He comforted her forlornness as she narrated her life's experience to him. He gave her some money, promised to call her whenever he has time's luxury and hinted that he has to leave now as he wanted to go before the road becomes really crazy.

Fateemah was happy that someone just showed her some kindness and not because he wanted to have sex with her. Kindness without an ulterior motive on a man's part was a rarity for her. No, it has almost never happened to her before.

He droves home with two voices in his head; the voice of the nurse and the story of Fateemah. The former he relished so much, the latter put him in a fix whether to believe it or not. He has heard many stories from different women.

One of his many girlfriends has shared her own experience as to how she became sexually incontinent; a nymphomaniac. Or just sexually promiscuous. Or just a woman with a sexual urge and a desire for intimacy with any understanding partner.

The lady revealed how she was taken advantage of by one of her uncles at age two; an uncle whom her parents had entrusted with her care when they both went to work very early in the morning and returned late in the night; all in a bid to earn a good living. They would come home late in the night, tired and with no time to share with her. Most of these times when they came back home, she was already asleep in her crib. The sexual molestation continued for a long time; many years. Some of it was such a fearsome blur. She grew to believe that she must have sex with the uncle every night until she was about age thirteen. Her misplaced guilt and fear of abandonment lasted for about ten years. The uncle never relented in all of that time.

When he heard that one story, he felt so sad that a man who was to be a guardian was the same person who grossly abused the very trust that he was supposed to protect. He prayed that if he were ever to have children, he wished for them to be boys. It was a selfish wish as he was not able to handle the intensity of the abuse that occurred to girls and women within his society. He should have been braver and teach his daughter to stand up to such abuse and turn potential heartache into strength.

He went straight home and found a note at his doorstep: *Am I now trash?* He knew immediately where that came from. The plus-sized colleague, of course. He tossed the note; a cruel affirmation of her suggestion.

THURSDAY. June Seventh, Two Thousand and Twelve. He woke up to a text message: *Hope you got home safe?* He wondered why that message came late. She ought to have asked that yesterday but he checked the time closely. She did send it yesterday but the interconnectivity networks of Global System for Mobile Communication (GSM) providers have been racing at below snail speed space of late. Anyway, he was happy that she has thought of him and he quickly responded: *Thank you for thinking of my safety. The message just got delivered, though. I hope that you will have a great day.*

He got up in preparation for the day. He was set to leave the house by 6AM so as to get things done as promptly as possible, especially the company's book has to be updated in order not to be found violating the bookkeeping rules. The company's auditors would usually come around unannounced, so one needed to keep abreast of his tasks, especially when it has to do with leading a team.

To his surprise, he opened his door to find his colleague at his doorstep. He did not bother to ask her how she got the keys to the gate. He was too experienced to engage in such talk. Many times he had given her the keys to his apartment when she had come to tidy up his place. She must have made a copy of the keys then. He concluded that it was high time he got the locks changed.

"You startled me." He said. Smilingly, she responded, "I just want to surprise you."

They have spent nights together but never has she come to his place this early. But he understood better now that a stalking game has been initiated. He understood women's ways and how to put them back in their place.

"I am off to work."

"Why so early?"

"I have to go do my logging. As you must have noticed, I left the office early yesterday". He just wanted to go around her and leave. There was work to do!

"Can we go inside before you leave?" She doesn't wait for an answer as she pulled off her shoes and walked on in.

"I am sorry, I have to go the office." He was willing to exit and leave her there.

"But we have to talk." She tried to stop him.

"Let's talk in the office." His mood was set for anything but to talk to her anywhere for the moment.

She has come in the hope that she would discover if he slept in the house with another woman. How else can he suddenly lose interest in giving her the daily tonic? Come to think of it, it's been two days past this moment that he has denied her access. But to her surprise, there was no girl with him. And the Let's-talk-in-the-office statement was so loaded because ordinarily, even when she has official things to discuss with him, they do it in his bedroom. Regardless of the nitpicking machinations of their involvement with one another and how they chose to handle the personal and professional details of that, he is done here.

As he took his usual trek to office he saw the police road block where he was harassed the previous day. The police recognized him and they greeted him as he walked pass by them. He acknowledged their collective greetings and he shook his head in pity at those who will be harassed, arrested, and exploited today.

Just as he got into his office, his phone beeped: *Thank you. I wish you a good day as well.* The response to the text he sent to the nurse came in. That's a good note to start the day? The choppy service was aggravating.

The lady colleague came to meet him in the office and as she came in, the security guys wondered why she came so early today, contrary to her typical tardiness. Even when she slept in her lover's house, they would come to the office separately to avoid the prying eyes of their colleagues. Not long after. Voices were heard.

"This is an office environment and if you must address me, do it with professionalism." He set the ground rules for now.

"It is me you are talking to."

"Of course, I am pointing my lips at you so it must be you am talking to." A bit of sarcasm leaked from his statement. Ha-ha, well, maybe more than a bit.

That was enough handwriting on the wall that they are kaput, done, over. He was tired of the difficulty, just as he has been tired of so many other ladies in the past. He got bored easily after sleeping with a woman for a little while. Not a wonderful quality but he was at least characterizing himself honestly.

He wanted to break new grounds. Explore new possibilities. One would wonder how such a man will be married once. What kind of stickem will there be for that partnership? The more reason he was scared of that hallowed institution. He has thought of having children by different women but not to get married to any of them. He subscribes to the idea that while he is not married to any of them they will not be able to query him. He may choose whomever, whenever, and it is no one's business but his own. Quite the philosophy, but will it work in a culture jealousy, and the demand that there be just one? He did not want to be a cheater once he got married.

She broke down in tears. He maintained his official mien as he continued working on his computer. She left his office but not without delivering barges of vituperations usual of a woman let go. He was not moved by her pleas or threats. He has quite a number of them that have never materialized beyond the saying of the words. He looked through his phone and reads the messages from the nurse again, over, and again.

Exactly an hour past midday, he called the sweet nurse. They both chatted as she was on her lunch break though attending to some things as they talked on the phone but she was positively engaged which drew his respect.

He hired a locksmith to change his locks. A good riddance to have- my-spare-key-without-permission, now ex-girlfriend. Impulsively, he sent a text to the nurse to inform her that he was changing his locks.

What happened to the old lock? Her response came quickly this time but instead of texting back he called her immediately and they chatted again about what happened. This was done with a satisfactory and peaceful feeling of sharing anything, including deep sheathed emotions, with a friend. Very relaxing. He hinted about Fateemah as well. She encouraged him to get in touch with her. He called Fateemah pronto. They agreed that she would come to his office the following day.

He happily sent a rejoinder text to the nurse: *She is not around but we will meet up tomorrow in my office.*

The nurse has a good heart. She was touched by the story of Fateemah and will be glad to help her. As a professional nurse, her responsibilities include counseling and rehabilitation.

FRIDAY. June Eighth, Two Thousand and Twelve. Fateemah left her friends behind in the shack at the beach side to keep her appointment with him. Thank goodness she will be riding opposite the heavy flow of traffic.

In the morning, people troop onto the island. So, the traffic to the island is usually huge on any working day of the week, while those exiting the island will have a jolly, smooth ride to the mainland. The reverse it is, in the evening.

She decked a native attire, one of the many beautiful designs the locals wear. It was a Friday and would people usually dress in native gear to signify the beginning of a weekend. That does not mean native clothing cannot be worn on any other day but most people still live like colonial slaves; anglicized, even to their breath. All-Day-All-Week-All-The-Time. Though there are some professions where one would have to dress smartly; those would be the Lawyers and similar professionals but even at that there are still smart native wears.

She was queenly in her native wear. The native designs, colors, and styles dignify and enhance all who wear them. African design is chic and comely at all times, regardless of race, color, or education.

He had quickly come to receive her at the reception when she called hinting him that she was around. He ushered her straight into his office without allowing her to sign the visitors register at the security desk in the office reception area. He deliberately came out to save her any embarrassment she may likely face if allowed to fill the register as one of the columns solicited her profession and definitely she could not honestly pen her trade in the book unless she was one of those shameless ones who do not give a damn about telling the world that they are ladies of the street. Also he doubted that she is that literate. They settled in to catch up as he offered her a cup of coffee.

"Your office dey nice."

"Thank you."

In her mind, she wondered what this well built; handsome professional might be up to, concerning himself with her. She staunched the flow of that thought with, *such is life*. Many leave houses of glass to dine with the dregs.

The coffee was brought in by the colleague and Fateemah greeted her having been introduced to one another at his place the other day.

"That is your girlfriend?" His colleague has just exited.

"My ex." He corrected her in no uncertain terms. She looked confused because she has only met her four days ago where she had been introduced as a girlfriend cum wifey. She gave him that look that intuitively elicits: *how come.*

"You were telling me something yesterday." He redirected her and to also remind her of her mission. That was not why she came there and to back off and mind her own business, jerk!

She started the story all over and, word for word, just as she said it the other day. Now he believed her because it is rare for a liar to remember every piece of his or her ramblings without betraying his or her stupidity. She told the story with the smoothness of a truth teller. It is her story, for real.

She had to start life all over again when she was framed by the woman who had introduced her into the trade. It was one of that woman's cohorts, a robber and member of a gang of robbers, who set the shed afire. She was again arrested and sexually molested while in the police cell by the officers; there had been no trial forthcoming at any point for her. But after several weeks an investigation revealed that she was not a member of any gang after all. It took that long in order for them to figure that out about her. She was let go with a strict warning not to return to the area and its margins either. She made up her mind to come to Lagos

Lagos is the dream city of many Nigerians and different nationals alike due to its economic importance serving as a commercial gateway to the whole of sub-Saharan Africa.

She joined one of the cattle transporters to the city after she had carefully asked and arranged with the driver. He suggested Agege because that was his own offloading port and convenient for both the driver and new found passenger. She agreed to go with him. But first, she paid with her body as there were no funds available for her to finance the trip.

While she was telling her story, the colleague pranced up and down the corridor as she could be seen through the see-through glass partitioning, for no obvious purpose. It was only obvious to him, though.

Fateemah continued her story. She got to Agege and had to stay in Oke-Koto with one of the cattle dealers whom she was introduced to by the driver of the truck. She would be the salesgirl and then sleep in the shed at night at the close of business. One evening, she was again ruffled by the area boys who had successfully trailed her for days and discovered that she was sleeping in the shed at night.

She saw rape as more of a way where men explore the world of having sex without paying for it. The experience was too common to her.

The *Sarkin Hausawa* of the cattle dealers made a pronouncement that no one should sleep in the cattle market henceforth, so as to avoid any clash with the host community; something to avoid as it had happened so many times in the past.

She had to secure a place in a brothel along Balogun Road, Agege, close to the Agege Pen-Cinema police station. One would have thought such would not be allowed so proximate to a police station since the law criminalized prostitution many years ago. In fact, there are two brothels along that same road nesting the police station.

Just as in the past, her trade was rosy because she was a new face and a youngster, about fifteen years old.

Soon after, a fight broke out in the brothel when two prostitutes fought over a certain client. They both accused one another of snatching each other's boyfriend. One would have wondered how prostitutes keep boyfriends. Common sense would have suggested that any man that goes into the brothel could go for any lady of his choice and fancy. There should be no permanent boyfriend or girlfriend in a brothel. Yet, they fought one another ferociously until the police from the Pen-Cinema station were called in by the brothel manager to quell the fracas. All prostitutes had to vacate the brothel as it was to be locked for some time so that peace and quiet could reign.

It is a game plan employed by the managers of such businesses. They explore implausible alibi to send sex providers out of their property after sometime so that new ones can be recruited. Many times, prostitutes are thrown out or even made to pay huge sums of money via police coercion if they default on the exorbitant rent charged them. The prostitutes pay daily, something amounting to about eighty percent of their income: a very exploitative trade.

Do the arithmetic here. How can one person receive money from eight men out of the ten that a prostitute sleeps with? The twenty percent that they are left with is used for their maintenance; condoms, tissue paper, fragrance, and other items including clothing and food. Only the desperate or the ill-informed go this route!

She had to look for an alternative since she had been asked to vacate the brothel alongside others. She was so fortunate to have one of her colleagues in the trade who suggested they pull their resources together so they could rent a cheap place and practice their trade where there would not have to be a grossly exploitative middleman to pay. They kept a hundred percent of whatever they made; no tax whatsoever either. They just had to pay rent to the landlord, monthly or annually, depending on the arrangement. They chose Aga as it was close to Pen Cinema area due to their known clientele. A good business decision. A career resilient decision.

Sukura was the friend who made the suggestion. Too bad they belonged to different camps now. She has been living in Aga for about four years now. She ended her story.

He listened to her entire story calmly. Never has he been so patient with anyone. He felt that he was a part of her story as they shared some significant similarities.

He had been sexually abused at four years old by a neighbor. Looking back, the woman must have been in her thirties at that time. Pedophiles, male or female, abound. He had his first sex at age six and ever since he has been active.

While growing up, his father had encouraged him to sow his wild oats near and far, reaching every corner of the world. Propagate one's own genes. Have some fun. He felt so sorry for her.

"After all of this, what do you want to do with your life?" He asked her.

"I ran away from home so that I could go to school!" Fateemah responded, looking confused. "But that is not yet to be as I have not been able to achieve that. Maybe I should have stayed back and gotten married in Niger."

He stood up, walked up to her chair, turned the chair so that she would face him and he looked her in the eye, "you can still go to school if you want to", he told her. She smiled as she listened to him. "But I am eighteen already and the last time I went to school was well over twelve years ago." She seemed confused at his offer. "If you are determined, you can do it." He convinced her and beamed at her a brotherly smile.

The colleague trotted into his office, saw them in that position, hissed as she stormed out instantly. In that instant, he asked the colleague, whose back was all that he could see now, "madam, how may I help you?" He sounded professional, not gruff.

"I will come back." She retorted as she finally closed the door. He smiled as he recalled the warning of one of his friends who had told him not to engage in any office romance as it would usually end in discord. He considered himself a grandmaster in female management and was sure of managing this one as well. Effortlessly.

While Fateemah was still with him, he sent a text to the nurse to inform her that they must have a long talk; a long talk per Fateemah's issue. He wanted to tell her the story of Fateemah and possibly work out a way to help her. But he really wished for a face-t0-face chat with her immediately. He was however being considerate of her schedule as he knew that there could a lot of mad dashing happening on Fridays.

As he got the delivery response from his phone he brought out some money and gave it to Fateemah. He encouraged her to try not to sell her body again because in all the years that she has been trading in bodily warmth she has nothing to show for it. And discreetly, he asked if she get to protect herself in all of her sexcapades, to which she gave a not too positive response. She would use protection normally but there have been many exceptions when a client would refuse to use a condom. He became a bit apprehensive. He just slept with her without protecting himself a few days ago and the last time he was screened for HIV was three months ago. But he calmed himself, believing that he will simply defer to the grace of God.

The Grace of God, when abused, will definitely not work where one goes into high risk situations such as unprotected sex with multiple partners. Only the devil can help an individual then. Even that may be out of his horned reach as well.

He assured her of his support and asked her to leave. He will let her know as soon as he worked out a plan to help her get back to school.

Fateemah hardly left the building when the colleague returned to his office and started yelling like some of the Nigerian politicians who have just lost an election.

"I knew that girl wasn't your sister when I saw her the other day." He looked at her straight in the eyes and wondered when he told her he meant it when she told her she was his sister. He also wondered when she started probing his relationships with others. He had told himself he would not promise any lady a wedding when he knew that he wouldn't stay in the marriage. More reason he would hardly lie when it comes to women affairs.

After much yelling, she left. He maintained his calmness. One of the ways to deal with any rancorous issue with anyone that is prone to eruption, is to remain silently calm for as long as possible. Frustrate their moves by not answering them. After all, the book of Proverbs says: Never answer a fool. It doesn't always work but is pretty effective typically.

His phone rang. The nurse has called to talk since he sounded urgent in the text. "It's not really something that we can talk about on the phone." He convinced her and they agreed to meet at Bar Beach on Sunday around 9AM.

Fateemah had thought of what he said to her. Could it be that he wanted to take her into a steady relationship? It would be good if that is his intention but she knew that he sounded more brotherly than as if he were a relationship seeking bloke. The words of admonition and encouragement kept coming back to her. No one has truly shown her any affection devoid of sex all her life. She felt that she should take to his words. At the least, she might just beg him to get her a job in his office. She herself was tired of the life of a prostitute. So many professional hazards abound, most significant of which is contracting HIV. She is aware of the disease but she, like many other women in the profession, are helpless. Many of them want a decent living but there is no help from anywhere and they do not know where or who to turn to. So they decide to use what they have to get what they need to survive in the harsh economy and society that is greatly fraught with massive inequality in the distribution of the nation's wealth.

Not that people want pity or a saccharine kindness from the government, all they ask from the stratagem of the politicians is to have some human sense about it and not to steal the commonwealth of the nation blind by self-enrichment. Corporate governance in government, public stimulus-response; servant-heartedness; respect for civic and civil rights, transparent leadership, probity, and equitable distribution of wealth; of all these, nothing is extraordinary in what the masses are asking for.

She made up her mind. She will try to stop the life; that life of a sex worker.

SATURDAY. June Ninth, Two Thousand and Twelve. The rescue mission surrounding the plane crash was to be brought to an end as announced in the news just as it was further stated that the corpses would have to be flown abroad for DNA tests to be done on them so as to identify the grossly charred corpses. The family members of the victims of the crash would have to come forward to receive the corpses of their loved ones after the results of the tests arrive from abroad. Also, the Dana Airways management will move to pay compensation to the victims affected by the crash. He listened to the news unperturbed because he knew nothing reasonable will come of the whole thing. There was no rationale for sending corpses so far away for something as simple as DNA analyses. It could be done in any corner of the world once necessary equipment and specimens are available. These politicians always find means to seek some gain however they can. Probably a favor was being paid back to some prior provisional provider in a foreign country.

He made plans to see some friends in the afternoon. He needed a break from girls.

By 11:25AM. His generator was still running, as there has been a blackout for over three days, then he heard someone trying to open his door. He quickly ran to see who it was through the peephole and he viewed his ex. He did not bother to open the door for her. It was stupid in the first place to make a copy of someone's key, no matter how close they may be to you, without their permission and even less wise to use the key to open the door from the outside when you knew that they could be inside of their house. That is not a surprise but absolute, open and unmitigated infringement.

As she discovered that the lock had been changed, she became agitated, wearing a melancholic look and then an outraged look. She started banging her fists on the door. He watched all the displays and to make matters worse for her, the more she banged the more he increased the volume of the song playing on the stereo. This time it was UB40's *Come Back Darling*. Neither he nor she is being very smart about this. She acted out and he goaded her some more; he enjoyed himself to the fullest with the live performance on the other side of the door lasting about thirty minutes. She tried calling him on the phone as well but he has blocked her number. That number that she used is now a nonstop dead end. She finally left when she recognized that all hope has been extinguished. After her departure, he quickly ran out, took his car and hit the town. He went visiting friends.

Boys talk as usual. They showed no surprise to a great showdown just experienced. They all laughed as they shared their experiences regarding women. Do women do the same? If not, they should.

One of them shared his when he was forced to tell one of his girls off. She had gone to lodge a complaint at the police station of being duped by him. Supposedly, he obtained money from her under false pretenses; that was her story. The police, without asking preliminary questions from her, foolishly followed her to carry out an arrest. When he was dragged to the police station and, being a lawyer, he confidently asked to see the Divisional Police Officer (DPO) of the station. He introduced himself as a Barrister-at-Law and his prayer was granted. He explained the whole situation to the DPO that the complainant used to be his girlfriend and the accusation of obtaining her funds under false pretenses that she accused him of, were the gifts and other items that she bought for him while they were dating. He was ready to return them to her as he knew a day like this might come. Therefore, he never touched any of those gifts and, instead, stockpiled them for quick return in a moment like this.

The DPO laughed and tried to reconcile them but they both refused all efforts. She insisted on getting all the gifts back from him and he was ready to return everything to her down to the most miniscule. The DPO jokingly added that the bodily warmth be returned too. The attorney laughed. The woman did not.

Some people can be difficult. If a relationship does not work for some reason, the two parties would do best to take it in good faith and go their separate ways maturely; maybe even remain as friends. Not all relationships lead to matrimony, as the saying goes.

He returned home tired but he has to prepare to keep his date for the next day. As etiquette-grounded lad, he made sure he called her to confirm the appointment.

"Yes, we will still meet tomorrow. God willing, 9AM."

"OK, goodnight."

He brought out and dusted off his shoes; a new pair of shoes that he bought at Gerber Square on Lagos Island.. Then got his well-starched plain sky blue short sleeved shirt and slim fit khaki colored chinos. This was only after he tried different combinations.

He took a cold shower and went to bed as the power has not been restored yet. He had to open up all the windows so that fresh air can freely breeze in without any blockage.

SUNDAY. June Tenth, Two Thousand and Twelve. He woke up early enough to wash his car, though it was not dirty. This was one date he has to be resplendent. And left the house early enough even though the hitch free, to-and-fro, of Lagos traffic on a, typical, Sunday. He wanted to be there before her so that he could watch her gaits as she walk up to him. Anxiety!

He got to the venue thirty minutes before time and secured a nice rendezvous site for them to sit, ordered a bottle of water and sipped it gently down his throat, giving a look of satisfaction like a man who has just taken down a bottle of Cristal.

And exactly 8:55AM, she touched his shoulder and that redeemed him from his daydreams. He was in eerie of how he was going to receive her as she walked up to him. But contrary to his mental image, he was caught unawares. He jerked up, startled by the sudden appearance of the real image by his side. He looked up and saw a belle beauty. Aisha Sessay of CNN could not even match her. She was wearing an above the knee navy blue dress, revealing her pretty, smooth shining legs, her pair of glasses so clean that they sharply reveal her shining eyes, even despite the time of day. She has very sweet dimples on her cheeks as she gave a pretty smile. A pair of silver gladiator sandals bedecked her feet. Then there was the matching small purse that she held in breathless anticipation. A beauty to behold! His heart leapt as he smelled her while embracing her to a warm welcome.

"Wow, you are astonishing; you have a very nice hairdo." She was wearing African- style plaits; one of the many that intensify the real beauty of a woman.

They settled into their seats and he beckoned a waiter to come around to take her order.

"What would you like?"

"Thank you. I will call you when I am ready." She was so courteous in telling the waiter not to bother for now. Very unlike many ladies who will talk rudely to anyone they perceive to be beneath their status.

They looked at one another for a moment with smiles on their faces. Then she broke the silence.

"You are a Muslim?" She asked with the common believe that many Christians would rather be in church on a Sunday morning.

"No! Why did you ask?"

"I thought you would be in church if you are a Christian."

"I am a Christian. Only that I am not a church-goer." He submitted this straightforwardly as not all believers choose to be churchgoers.

"How do you mean?"Then he started a narration. "Many people have asked what my locus in talking about this issue is; well I was born into a Christian home. Some may probe further and say that is not enough; they will ask if I have a personal relationship with Christ; well I can tell you I have a relationship with Him that is why I have the boldness to talk like this. The boldness that I have to say I am a Christian comes from the understanding that I don't need any other appellation, be it a prefix or a suffix to establish what being Christ-like means. I know He is not a noisemaker. The question, "are you a born again Christian?" has been so abused that it is fast loosing not only its original connotation but its appeal as well. Christianity is a way of life patterned after the life and teachings of Christ. It is not a religion. It is either you are a follower of Jesus Christ or not, no midway to it. The different doctrines being employed by various kinds of people and organizations today were part of the symbological veil that Christ Himself shredded when He cried with a loud voice before yielding up the ghost on the cross. Having established that let me come to the fore. I encountered a sick friend lately; sick in the real sense of it. This friend of mine was ill and was placed on medications so I checked on him to know how he was faring. I asked if he was taking his medications as prescribed, and also if he was eating well. I felt so disappointed when this supposedly educated guy told me he is fasting and taking medications at the same time. I really felt like flogging this guy so badly but I had to respect his sense of want. He said "Our Pastor declared a 100day fast". A song by that supernal being, Fela Anikulapo-Kuti came to mind: MR. FOLLOW FOLLOW.

Christianity is fast being reduced to churchism. Laodiceanic. An every Sunday social fad to show off one's currency to neighbors, family and friends or as a political or economic tool. Contrary to the primary purpose of going to a place of worship of the Almighty God, a place to learn more about the principles of being Christ-like, a church is now becoming another convergence of fun-seekers. My friend in the above scenario is a churchist.

VOICES IN THE CATHEDRAL

Praise the Lord.
Hallelujah!
The Lord is good to us today,
Hallelujah!
Drop your offering.
Hallelujah!

So awed at how every Tom, Dick and Harry clamors to wear the cassock, claiming they are "yielding to the call' but in the real sense, they are propelled by their business acumen because of the so many appurtenances like tithes, offerings and other levies that come into the house of the Lord. We have many cases at hand. Take a walk to any Magistrate court in the land and you will be bewildered at what these so-called MoG and WoG are standing trial for.

The recent must-build-a-university craze embarked on by some faddist leaders, inadvertently levying church goers inevitable is putting the church in a derogatory *qui vive*. There is nothing wrong in churches establishing universities, in fact, most prestigious institutions of learning in the world sprung up from the initiatives of the church, but when they are established by public funds they should be made accessible and affordable to the public. Majority of these private universities were built by levies and contributions of church goers who were mostly psyched to donate to a good cause, however when the universities are finally established, the same church members pay through their nostrils if they choose to send their wards there and many are not even able to send their wards to such schools because of the high fees."

He continued the narration of a very good friend of his who told him how a pastor in his area had embarked on a poverty alleviation/reduction program.

The Pastor started out by selling handkerchiefs and wrist bands to his congregation. After a while that he had gathered enough money he went on to purchase about 2000 units of motorcycle. He cut a good deal since he bought in bulk and he was ready to give one to any member of his congregation who was willing to go into Okada business. Ordinarily, the delivery in such a business is a thousand naira pd but our Pastor friend was willing to collect just a thousand pm for the next 24months which would amount to twenty-four thousand naira after which the rider will become the owner of the bike.

One would have quickly interjected and said that was a good one. But his friend made him understand some facts as the Pastor is so smart and indeed deserves to be nominated for a business award.

First, if there is any issue of loyalty amongst the church members, the followers that took the Okada will, ordinarily, stick with the Pastor, come rain come shine because that is where their prayers for an end to poverty is supposedly answered.

Now let us acivate our arithmetic acumen.

If an Okada operator makes about three thousand naira per day, the tenth of that goes to the church as tithes, multiplied by the number of days in twenty four months. This is not to mention offerings which come as the spirit leads, and seeds of different kinds, plus the installments they will have to pay over twenty-four months. Mehn! Those guys would have been better off if they were told outrightly they are in a slave camp

She laughed uncontrollably at this analysis but that is the truth.

Christianity is not a religion; it is a relationship that we have come to inherit through Jesus Christ that came into the world to die for our sins, which signify sacrifice that springs from divine love, so that we can be reconnected to the Almighty God.

Where is the love and sacrifice when Pastors chose private jets above of a lot waiting to be done to make this society of ours a better place in terms of social responsibility? Why are our Pastors not just telling the truth and nothing but the truth? Maybe they need to tell more truth, some people will argue; whichever. Let them tell the truth to every leader under their ministration that public funds should not be stolen. Let them refuse to accept tithes paid from people of questionable wealth, as the Lord frowns at such practice. Let them make it known to their aides that front seats should not just be for the VIPs: to sit in front with the Overseer of a certain mega church comes at a cost. Let them know that the crucifix is now seen as another bodily adornment but our Christian living is the model we have to show off not the ostentation of being called a Pastor. I repeat; Jesus is never a noisemaker.

I am not a hypocrite. That is why I don't go to church like every other church- goer. More so, our hearts are the temple of the Lord and He doesn't look at our nodding heads or vacuous shouts for His attention. If you like call me an atheist. But I am not against the convergence of the people of God of whichever denomination. In fact, I do not joke with worshiping God everyday.

However, far and beyond worshiping God within a constructed frame, or hitting your head on the ground with highly expressive tendency of nihilism as a form of His worship because you want your religion to be seen as superb, while your heart is filled with so much hatred and thirst for blood. Try and know that your heart should be His throne because that is the sanctuary He inhabits, just as it has been from the days of old, and not your religion. Open up and cut a personal deal with

Him. A child does not need a third party to talk to his/her parents if the relationship works. Jesus even admonished us to know the truth so that we can be free."

He expressed his views so passionately. She almost could not help but nodded in agreement with his opinions. Coincidentally, it helped that she happened to share those very same views. She was quietly impassioned herself. "But that does not mean we should abandon the works we have been commissioned to do." She posited.

He is curious. "What works might that be?"

"Preaching the gospel. Can you tell me about your relationship?" She was unintentionally imprecise.

"If given an exercise book, I can fill it with the names of different women that I have been with." He mistook her question to mean his relationships with women. Whereas she asked about his relationship with God. Possibly, it had been intentional. "Why are you like that?" She asked that with a sincerely probing smile.

He responded that he was exposed to sex at a very tender age. He had uncles who would send him to their girlfriends and who would sleep with the girlfriends in his presence at about the tender age of six.

He made his first try in his primary school days. He followed the girl who had gone into the shared toilet and he went in with her.

Who would have thought that children of that age would have been engaging in sexual activity and that separate toilets for them might be a wise idea?

His first ejaculation was when he was about nine when he returned to the woman who had abused him originally. He jumped up when he saw the fluid fly from his manhood, the woman laughed and told him not to worry, that he was now a man and asked him to cum again. Then and there he understood what it meant to reach climax, and also to go on rounds of sex.

The more disgraceful thing that he was not proud to say he was involved in was a date rape. But all the same, he spoke about it. Yet his eyes lost all of their vigor when he spoke about that act. He wished that he could travel back in time to rewrite the story now that he understood how barbaric, irresponsible, criminal, and inhumane rape was. He wished that he could see that girl and apologize for the wrong he had done to her.

She interrupted him when she saw his tone slide down.

"I have been raped before."

He raised his head rapidly and the skin on his forehead crinkled.

She was raped at the age of twelve.

Why in some regions of the world does rape almost seem like a rite of passage and a commonplace happening?

Two boys who had been troubling her in their neighborhood, pounced on her one evening at about 9PM, as she was on her way home from church where she had attended an evening Mass. She was practically torn through by the two boys, both five years her senior. She returned home crying to her parents. They were not educated, though they were enlightened enough to know that the first thing to do was to go to a police station to file a complaint. Immediately afterwards, she was taken for a medical examination.

She said this without losing any sense of her pride. She had carried the pain for a long time, but later overcame it all after much counseling.

Many women died inwardly in agonizing pain after being raped. They sheltered the secret, the shame burning a hole in their psyche, because they were so frightened, feeling almost poleaxed, to tell the world that they had been raped.

Just as a doctor illustrated, "would you not go to the Police station and possibly let the world know that you had been robbed or attacked by a robber? That must be applied to the situation of rape as well." Shout it out! Lodge a complaint in a nearby police station. Seek medical and psychological help. It's nothing to be ashamed of. And if the culture stigmatizes you, what then? Bravery as stigma? Then it was only to be perceived as society's perception that was wrong. But society carries such a weight.: Horrible when wrong, wonderful when right.

He went on his knees and apologized for the act.

"Why are you apologizing for what you didn't do?" She asked him this gravely, in true consternation.

"I am using you as a point of contact for the lady that l acted rudely with", still on his knees. She held him up and said, "OK." They both smiled then. She is his lightning rod.

"Will you make your order now?" He hoped so. He is ready to move on from the subject at hand.

She stood up, stretched her left arm to him and pulled him up to walk with her as she led him to the car lot. She dipped her right arm into her purse and brought out a car key and pressed it to deactivate the security lock of an automobile. The car that responded was the current model of one of the leading car manufacturing companies in the world. She opened the trunk to get some small chops; kebab and the likes and some drinks as well. He looked at her with some awe. The way they appeared, they were homemade

"Why did you stress yourself to do that?"

"I know things are expensive here, so I decided to do this to save you any difficulty." Her smile was quietly radiant. This was who this woman was. A reasonable woman is also a good manager.

"It is no stress for me." He boasted but it came out flat.

"Well, I will have to make you pay for the chops and my stress then."

"How much?" He was capable and he wished to show that to her.

"For the chops, it is ten naira, and for the stress, you will have to just say, thank you." She jokingly bended as if waiting for someone to appreciate her.

Truly, not all women are fastidious. They just want men to show some appreciation for their efforts, even just a simple thank you. Thank you all-around is a wonderful thing. Make them plentiful to subordinates too.

"My heart pounded. I thought you were going to ask for millions for your stress." He laughed, and then genuflected as he said his thankyous to her.

They laughed as they occupied the back seat of her car, settling down to do justice to the chops.

He told her the entire story of Fateemah and how she would like to get education but lacking the wherewithal. He became so impassioned in his desire to help Fateemah but he did not know how.

"What is your plan to help her?"

"I want to finance her education."

She laughed as he said the last statement. She made him realize that it is far better to teach someone to fish than to feed them fish. Make them independent and watch them do wonders.

She suggested that it is better to get her a job. She would talk to the head of the Human Resources department in the hospital where she works to see if she could be drafted into the hospital as an aid, and then, whatever she earns will contribute to her education. They both agreed to take her as their sister. She will be made to go through an HIV screening in order to determine her status in one of the available Voluntary Counseling and Testing Centers (VCT) scattered over each and every corner of the city; offering their services for free to the public. She will have to be put on drugs for treatment and management of HIV if clinically determined that she is carrying the virus. Medicine has achieved the ability to give an HIV positive individual a very normal life where goals can be achieved over a span of healthy years. Thank goodness the stigmatization of people with HIV is fast being reduced as people are getting more and more enlightened every day.

He will continue with his quarterly checks.

The nurse was ready to take Fateemah into her apartment so as to take her off the street. Willy-nilly, the time will come when her body will age and no cosmetics will be able to allow her profitability in the sex industry. So how would she earn a living by then? And yet, the biggest question was, why would she ever desire a lifetime of prostitution anyhow?

Stanley is the name of the guy, and Sumbo, is the nurse. Both felt happier that they were able to affect a life positively.

She pulled off her shoes so that she could enjoy the tingly sensation of the beach sand directly under her feet. They walked the beach hand in hand like the two jolly friends that they actually have grown to become in this shortest period of their meeting. He was in his mid-thirties. She was in her late thirties.

Fateemah was informed of their decision and she rushed to meet them at the beach. She has been celibate for the past two days. That was huge. She has signaled that the lifestyle of the sex trade is behind her.

It is never too late. This is life, none other.

SELF DISCOVERY

Unbeknownst tilts down knowledge.
The human reference revere naught.
Food. Clothes. Shelter.
The necessitio-essentialism.
A lot gone far gross gain.
Immoderation appurtenances we exalt .
In oblivion exterminate essence.
Through oblivion we gain purpose.
Simplicity is null.
Simplicity is all.
Long gone clandestinely unpristine.
Tearing at peaceful marauders.
A service to savagery.
Opiumsmic grasp on the chord of breath.
Boomerang implosion.
Confluencing each and all of our paths.
The journey back home,
Enjoyfully limitless.
The way to self-detoxification.

SOCIETAL FRAGMENTS

CRIES OF AGONY

"Nobody deserted you! You need to face the fact of life on your own." Those were the exact words one of his friends used.

A man is born into this life from the copulation of two other beings, resulting in the fetus forming in the belly of a sweet mother. But the fact still remains that at a certain point in that child's life, he is left all alone to surmount the challenges he must face in that life in a world full of intrigues, uncertainties and hopes.

Hope. It is usually the dusk of emptiness, the dawn of a mirage of a better tomorrow. And those hopes contain the belief that someday the threshold of fortune will swing to one's side. The assurance and reassurance of destiny in the hands of the gods usually bring false expectations, often.

Alas! The door swung shut to bring the reality of the words of his friend home. Looking at his surroundings, he saw that truly he was to face his all and all alone.

"Good Morning, Ma", the teacher was greeted as she entered the classroom. This was the routine. "All seated", she ordered.

It was the start of a new week, so everyone was still looking relaxed and neat but eagerly looking forward to the end of the week, already. That was the only time they got respite of seemingly escape from the wrench of fear that followed any form of insolence on the part of the students. The students feared that very possible discipline. And it was a great treat to the teachers, for their day was not complete until one punishment or the other was doled out to any scapegoat that crossed their path.

And he, being one of the most brilliant of his set, kept to the right angular section of the entrance of the class, where he had a vast view of the blackboard without impediment, and he could also hear every sigh that the teacher may make. That has always been his positioning from Junior Class and even when he became a big boy in form four where he could be proud enough to wear his brown pair of trousers with the turn-up edges along with his white and brown stripe short sleeve shirt. All, well-ironed during the weekend at the finish of all the household chores; in preparation, ahead, for the new week, and neatly hung at the nail stake holding all the other school items, including his school bag. All assignments, double-checked for errors. No wonder he was an A plus student at all times. The first and last time he came third in the class, he went home somber and that sobriety lasted for weeks: his mother and siblings were worried about his indifference to the things around him, wondering what was on his mind but nobody asked him anything.

"I have always done well. How come I came in third this term?" He spoke to the man in the mirror.

The girl that came in first was just transferred from a private school. She has to come here because her primary health worker parents were transferred to the district. The other girl had always been his classmate from form one. She was one of the girls that got stuck to the backseat. In his estimation, she was lousily irresponsible, subjective as well.

It was permissible that students or members of staff could wait to engage in some academic endeavor on their own. But the allotted time for this endeavor must not exceed one hundred and forty five minutes in time, else, any second outside of this parameter amounts to a trespass upon the school property, and anyone observed violating this rule is liable and is considered a violator.

Hungry and tired, he strolled through the veranda of the staff room after the close of the school activities He looked through into one of the rooms through and saw images. Yes. It was the teacher and the lousy lady that came second. They were by themselves in the expanse of the teachers' room. She was sitting on the table and he was standing close to her. He quickly bent his head below the level of the window to avoid being seen by the lovebirds. *No wonder she came in second.* This thought rattled his mind as he walked home. The reality of his immediate environment came alive to him for the first time.

*****

"You are on grade level thirteen, step three of the Federal Government Civil Service, and you still cannot afford to take your kids to a private school. Needless to say, there is absolutely no way of taking your family on a trip to a resort. How are your friends that are even below you in ranking making things happen for their own families? You are only man in the room and that is not the wholesome definition of a man." His wife rattled on and on.

What does one expect from a civil service that is fast losing its civility?

They have been dating since their university days, right from their sophomore year. She saw a brilliant young man with a brighter future than others because he was always atop the class with a peerless CGPA; that was academics par excellence, a very solid feat to have accomplished amongst his contemporaries. She worked her way into his heart by hook and by crook. She made sure that she gave him all of the warmth and friendliness a man may be looking for in a lady; but all of these were with the highest ulterior motive of winning him all to herself so that he could, in turn, help her with her class assignments and tests. No doubt she was a beauty to behold; but cunning, insightful, and above all, agile. Being foxy is what most women need to succeed nowadays.

"What am I to do?" He snapped this question out to himself.

Homecoming for him was usually with its attendant headache. Most times he would stay back in the office at the close of work, in the company of like minds, men who derive pleasure in their separation from their wives and kids. They all would stay back together in the office discussing politics and the reforms of the government of the day. Arguments and counter-arguments.True Federalism and Resource control. The fiscal sharing formula. The neglect of oil producing regions leading to hostility between the host communities and the oil companies. The environmental degradation. International Relations. And lately, the emergence of various sects that have become a cramp on our security situation making us popular for the most wrongful of reasons.

These were all common features of their discussions. These were knowledgeable and seasoned experts if one was to judge by their in-depth analyses. Most often though, the subject matter was of their sojourn through the cycle of life that landed them in their present state of marital quandary.

"I should not have married her. But she said she was pregnant. I had to see it through with her because I was the one who deflowered her. So I took pity on her and took her in. Now, see what she is making my life go through; hell and beyond." One of them rhetorically stated amidst his drunkenness.

"They warned me; warned me that I should not marry her. But I ignored their warnings and pleas. Family and friends warned me. See where I am now." Another chipped in.

"My wife is a popular name amongst the men in the neighborhood. They know her just as they would the back of their hands." Another joined in the progressing conversation, drunk. "The bachelors and the married men in the neighborhood know her well." He was sorrowful as he talked to his colleagues.

Marital infidelity is usually a painful and undesirable topic to play upon. Infidelity is the bane of so many broken marriages lately. It is so destructive that the aftershock on generations to come cannot be underestimated.

*****

He would habitually come home at his usual odd hour, late night. All he can do was to barely stagger into the room and wait till the dawn of a new day. The whole night's sleep was to him as just a few minutes as his mind was occasionally preoccupied with a ceaseless flow of thoughts. His friend's words came drifting to his mind, leaving him so restless all through the night.

His wife looked at him because tonight was different; his usual snoring and dead-log posture vanished. She wondered the cause, but she never made a sound about it; they have had a strained relationship for some months now and for her to venture into his odyssey would be risky. She might just meet the same cold indifference typical of months back. She kept to herself because she did not want to create a flare of anger from her heartthrob.

The sun has fully risen, bringing to him his happy mood, for yes; it is the perennial escape from home again.

If perchance he happened to screw up waking up on time his day will be ill-starred. His robotic response to the chiming of the clock; an addiction that grew over a decade. It became a necessity with the influx of people into his part of the town. Hitherto, the hinterland was so calm that any guest would wonder if life existed outside the house they have gone to visit. With time, a change of destiny brought about by rampant inflation, people were driven into the suburbs because rents seemed relatively cheap there. It was well over two decades now. Rents were still cheap compared to the cities but the associated sanity in the suburbs was no more. The way to the office was a boisterous one. It ought to be a forty-five minute drive, but if he should delay by a second then he has to go through a two-hour hectic driving with bashing and cursing as part of it. Torture.

"We will only have to wake up so early in order to make it to work and other places in good time." The hinterlanders gave their retort.

The state master plan, brazenly shoved into the face of any builder in the seventies and early eighties, has been tossed resulting in odd and deficient assortments: a hospital on a dumpsite around a church occupying a motel adjacent a mosque beside a pen of pigs directly opposite an eatery close to a public toilet in a marketplace inside an army cantonment. The definition of a veritable slum.

*****

"I am confused. I am between two women; my dream girl and my wife," one of the men said. He was filled with a bittersweetness; excited and sad, all at once.

He has been married for eight years and he has three children with his wife. His wife was a modestly pretty ebony lady. "You do not need much money to maintain the skin of your wife." His friends would jokingly tell him, "just get her original Shea butter or olive oil and she will remain shining and smooth."

"She is God-sent, taking care of the home front especially, and the kids, without me having to contribute a dime most times." Those were his words a few months before he met his dream girl.

An emotional man cannot be totally trusted. He sways with his emotions, easily blown by the wind. He changes his decisions just as the direction of a ship changes by the whim and caprice of a heavy thunderstorm. One time he is a love slave; the other time he is a viper.

"Wow!" One of the friends exclaimed at the introduction of the dreamgirl. Beautiful. Elegant. Gorgeous. The epitome of beauty. The paradigm of womanhood. Alluring. These words freely used at her reception into their midst in one of their outings at their usual pub.

"Have you told her you are married with kids?" One of his buddies asked this as he shoved him aside to keep his words away from the dream girl's hearing.

"No!" He responded very quickly while covering the interrogator's mouth with his arm, "I want us to be so engrossed in one another before any other thing is established. I am not sure about her stance yet. Only afterwards will I break the news. At that point, she will have no choice other than to take it as it is." Quite a good move, his listeners decided. One would have thought that divorce was inevitable so that he might move on when asked what he would do with his wife, "I do not know yet", he was indeed a confused man, "she has been a peaceful and responsible woman all the period that I have known her so I have no rationale to throw her out. Moreover, she takes care of the kids so perfectly that no other woman will be able to do same. No logical case for infidelity in the minutest form could be established against her. So I have no excuse for wanting to file papers for dissolution." His friends noticed his confusion and they all steered clear of the subject as they were loathed to lose a friend by talking rudely about his wife or dream girl. Indifferent. Taking no sides.

Typical of men. They want to bite two or more significant chunks off at the same time; usually ending up with multiple crises at their doorstep for the effort. One of them had said, "why do we men usually go about placing our heads into hornet's nests? Were my wife a peaceful woman, highly responsible, and faithful, then I would have no reason to go chasing after another woman. Or multiple women, for that matter." What a groundbreaking concept that a wife might be the perfect and only partner needed.

*****

Weekday or a weekend, his system has routinely adjusted to the 6AM clock chime. He took a time out from the boys hangout this weekend and as he watched his own children play, he longed for his own childhood again.

His father died when he was about seven months old leaving him and his four older siblings: three boys and a girl. The man died working as a traffic marshal. His life ended as a merciless truck driver ran him over; a hit-and-run case.

His father's portrait was hung on the wall of their room. He had on a peaked cap, dude blue shirt, and his black pair of trousers while standing in a salutation posture with his right arm elegantly touching the peak of the tipped cap. Many times as a young lad, he had wondered how painful this posture must have been on his arm. The man seemed a dutiful man. He could tell from the portrait. He never blinked in the line of duty.

He recollected how playful he once was with his collection of cans that he could build into a moving car with four cans as its wheels. Sometimes he carved out a log for a lorry carrying other things on its back, framed with cardboard on each side of the lorry's carriage space. Above all, he remembered how prudish he could be.

His mother had warned him that if he should wander too close to a girl, she would become pregnant and both of them would have to leave their present vicinity for a faraway place where they knew no one and must start a life, harder and fiercer than what they were experiencing in their present locale. She would speech the same to her only daughter. Her own admonishments were harder and flatter than the boys. She terrified the children. "You will be pregnant and turn into an outcast in this life and the ones to come. For an eternity, so shall your suffering be." She sternly told her without ever holding anything back. She took them then to a church nearby to a matinee to sharpen their moral standing.

He recalled one of those moments.

JUST ONE MORE

ACT I

At a drinking joint, built with palm fronds; Abebi, the palm wine seller is sitting beside a table with bottles of different concoctions. A small shelf also contains different brands of cigarettes. Olakunle, Adeoti, and some other men are in the joint drinking and prattling.

Olakunle: Yesterday, I drank two cartons of Biggie, after three shots of Monkey tail, two shots of Opa eyin. That yesterday was no good.

Adeoti: You better dey take am jeje. Awuf dey kill person. You were just drinking as you see am that yesterday. If no be me wey come carry you, you for sleep for gutter. Na there you for dey live.

(They burst into laughter.)

Olakunle: Na lie. You don see where fowl die through leg injury?

Adeoti: Just dey do am jeje o.

Olakunle: Today, I wan drink like sey na Christmas. I go take seven shots of white and come add am baba dudu put. You know Akanni talk sey make

we meet am for Iya Olobe junction
later.

(They have been at the joint all day and it is getting dark already. People are already leaving or their homes. Olakunle is visibly drunk now.)

Olakunle: Abebi, give me Gold.*(Abebi quickly runs to her table to get a pack of cigarettes and gives it to Olakunle.)*

Thank you, good woman. I am going to take
you from that useless man that calls himself
your husband.*(Olakunle tries to touch Abebi and she moves back so quickly.)*

Abebi: Don't touch me o. You know I am a
married woman.*(Olakunle reaches out the more to touch Abebi.)*

Olakunle: I told you I like these your two face and
Idibia.

Abebi : *(Slaps Olakunle)* I said don't touch me.

Olakunle: *(Visibly staggering and touching his chest.)* Me.
(Pounces on the woman with several punches. Abebi falls fainting to the ground.)

Adeoti: *(Checks the pulse of Abebi.)* Lakunle,
Yepa! She is no more breathing. I think
she is dead.

(Fear and pandemonium rent the air.)

Olakunle: Please help me. Mogbe! *(Arms on the head now.)(A Policeman appears at the scene.)*

Policeman: Where is the man?

(Olakunle is whisked away by the police.)

ACT II

(Dokun is standing and waiting outside for someone.)

Dokun: This girl should come quick now. I have
         other runs to fix. *(Andrew walks in on him.)*
Andrew: O boy! Why are you pacing all around
          the place?
Dokun: I just got a new catch yesterday and she
          is checking on me in few minutes. Am
          fully prepared for her.*(Shows his macho)*
Andrew: Ah! Again. *(Mouth opens wide.)* Just take am
           easy o. What about Bisi and her friend?
           They had a showdown here the other day
           when they met here. I remember the
           twins and their mother. Na free for all.
           Guy, everybody don know you for this
           neighborhood as badoooo.
Dokun: That one small. Yetunde and her cousin
           including their neighbor. That day come
           see live Royal Rumbles here *(A lady passes
           by while they talk. She is seductively dressed.
           Dokun immediately abandons Andrew.)*
Dokun: Excuse me, pretty lady. I am a gentleman of
           great passion and vision. I have been
           telescoping you as you traverse this
           territorial plane for some time and I must
           confess you are indeed a paradigm of
           beauty, an epitome of excellence and a
           delight of every man. In fact, you are a
           model to all Arabian princesses. May I
           know your cognomen please?
Augustina:*(Smiling.)* My name is Augustina.
Dokun: What a pretty name for a pretty damsel like
            you. Augustina! I am not a flatterer, am
            just stating the obvious. I will be highly
            honored if I can show you my abode.

Augustina: Maybe next time as I am in a hurry now.

Dokun: *(On his knees.)* I know you are out on a
purpose but I will be glad if you just see
my place briefly. P-L-E-A-S-E.

(Immediately , Dokun leads the way and Augustina follows.)

Andrew: *(Looks on.)* Dokun I am still here o.

Dokun: Andy baba, abeg, I need to entertain my
guest and I be out in ten minutes. *(Winks at
him.)* *(A few minutes later he comes out in a wrapper.)*

Dokun: The lady is sweet. *(Andrew laughs.)* I
am a hero. This is number two hundred
and one.

   (Dokun crows unconsciously as he talks on.)

 Andrew: Is that a new style in town?

Dokun: That is a nice one but I can do better.

   (He crows again.)

Andrew: Dis one no be normal thing again o.

  (Holding Dokun and cautioning him to stop the frenzy.)

Dokun: Please let me do one more.

 *(While this is going on Augustina runs out of the house.
Dokun crows the last time and goes lifeless.)*

ACT III

SCENE I

(Jack walks in jubilating.)

Jack: I told Shina that I will disgrace that
    Adebutu Kessington man. He thinks he is
    smart. Ijebu man to the core.

(Shina walks in, joins in his jubilation as they both lift one another shouting.)

Shina: I am a friend of a champion. Jacko, you
    go find something for me o.

Jack: No worry. You know I never lose for this
    game. If I know I for nab that single two
    join zero and nine. If na that one I play
    Baba Ijebu for go back village today.
                    (They both walk out.)

SCENE II

(Jack displays his new affluence.)

Jack: Thank God for His favor. Baba Ose Oku
    itoju mi.*(He sings and dances then a preacher walks in.)*

Bose: Brother Jack, we didn't see you in church
    last week. What happened?

Jack: Sister Bose, I won a jackpot last week and we
    had fun all weekend. I will come this Sunday.
    I even want to give up all of this messy
    lifestyle. To tell you the truth, God has been
    so gracious to me.

Bose: Thank God that you know He is gracious. It
    is a right step in the right direction. I pray you
    don't go back. *(They join hands and pray and she leaves.)*

Jack:*(Soliloquizing)* Of a truth, God has been so
    good. I will serve Him. *(He sits)*But come to

think of it, if I become fully born again now I no go dey play Baba Ijebu again. Anyway, my God is a good God. He will provide for me according to His riches in glory. (*Pacing through the room.*) Ok, I know what to do. I will borrow from neighbors then sell all these stuffs. The chedah wey I get I go nab am for two direct. I know sey if I do this last one I go hit big money then born again go sweet well. God I thank you for this wisdom.(*He leaves jubilating.*)

SCENE III

(*He comes back crying*)

Jack: I don enta gbese. See wetin I put myself into. (*Brings out a list from his pocket.*) I borrow 50k from Baba Bili to pay back 65k, 20k from Aliu to pay back 25k, 3kfrom Segun to pay back 5k, Iya Tosin 33k to pay back 40k, 70k from Kudi to pay back 90k…Yeh!Mogbe!! Morogo!!! See wetin ojukokoro cause me o…

(*Neighbors come in and hold him, demanding their money and they drag him out!*)

End

They lived a most well-cultured life. Virginity was a treasure to be bestowed upon one's matrimony, and sex a proprietary aspect of marriage and marriage alone. Not that which has become the norm in today's society. The erosion of values is the bane of the increasing problems in our present society. And the problem just goes deeper and deeper as time goes on, West or East, the same problems exist everywhere.

With her strict indoctrination, none of her children were caught engaging in any childish pranks like going into a dark corner with the opposite sex. They were studious and obedient to her instructions.

Who can blame such a woman? A widow faced with the upkeep of five kids from the sale of petty stuffs by the roadside.

The fight to survive is what no one desires to lose. The struggle is an everyday thing. Even when the results are not sufficient, the need to survive brings an inherent strength to the fore.

She was a full time housewife while her husband worked and provided everything they needed in the house to the minutest of the minute. He enjoyed pampering his family and presently, things were occasionally affordable with whatever he was earning. Her friends had told her to put aside part of the money she got as a monthly allowance to start a small petty trading that would, in turn, add to her family's economy. They let her know that it was not good for a woman to be idle. Anything could happen. At the least, she should be able to contribute a fraction to the financial obligations of the family as the helpmate that she was created to be. She shrugged off the suggestions initially but, thank goodness, she finally heeded them. Not long after she started the petty trading, her husband was run over while at his work. And not long after her husband's demise, her in-laws abandoned her to her fate. They had promised to take care of the kids, help with their upkeep, especially their education. But all of that was shown to be lies. Not one of them showed up again. It would have been a different case if her husband had left something behind: properties, stocks, money, investments of any kind. Instead, he only bequeathed a burden to them. One of the man's distant cousins said this secretly.

She would set out very early in the morning, one of the early risers in the district, to display her wares before all the others on the road leading to the school. Those wares mostly consisted of lozenges and stationeries. She first cooked the day's meal and then had those plates rest in a warmer which she had inherited from her mother. She doled out the instructions. This included the time each meal was to be taken and where to go get the food since she knew that all of her kids were adherents to her rules.

She would set out so early and was back in the late evening. But she would stay back at home on weekends since her patrons needed no tutoring on Saturdays or Sundays. Her weekends were spent telling stories of gallant deeds of their late father.

"He was a brave man."

He grew to admire his father through his mother's stories and his gallant portrait.

*****

Politics is an interesting discipline. To some, it is a job and to others it as a vocation. Regardless of how they view themselves within that field, politicians are people who you help make their own dreams come true but, in turn, they turn around and shatter yours, especially, when the respect for the rule of law is only mirrored in their smiles. Their characters are typically questionable. They are like those Christians holding on to their faith only on Sundays but go about the week heartless as rabid dogs. For the heart pricked, those with hearts, it was a no-go zone.

It would be a general election in few months. Political jingles, rallies, campaigns, debates, accusations, counter-accusations, backbiting, backstabbing, blackmailing, alliances, accords, coalitions, even intrigues used in hoisting and ousting one another. These are elements of this period, especially when there are so many questionable candidates jostling for political posts.

"Vote for us! We are the reformists! We will Joshua you to the Promised Land and that is why we are giving you the new Messiah who will steer the wheels directly to Canaan." All of the hyperbolic shouting here and there.

They sound so sweetly close to the people as they present the challenges that people face in their daily lives. They promise to tackle all of these issues in their talk with out-of-this-world solutions to ageless, deeply entrenched problems. Promises they will never keep. They even promise, within two weeks of their assumption of or resumption in office, babies to childless women. Even the intelligentsia fall for their sugar- coated tongue. So how intelligent does that make the intelligentsia?

He met one of the office seekers on his street when they came one Sunday morning before he set out; weekends were usually boring to him so he chose to stay in the company of his boys till late in the night. The politician had come to campaign in the district, going from street-to-street selling his views to the people of the grassroots.

"What are your programs to redeem our continuing pariah state from further abyss, Mr. Honorable?" He pressed the politician on that one.

"We are still moving slowly due to the archaic ways of the former system, which is controlled by the people who bask in the security of the now but fear to venture into the new." The politician still had more to say, "we must obliterate such from our system." They both nodded their heads in the affirmative. They shared some things in common believing themselves as the new generation. The old politicians have sucked on the teat of glory too long.

Because of our accented politics of godfatherism which we have become used to as part and parcel of our political existence, we throw away all principles of democracy, intra and inter parties ideals, and are just playing dummies to the whims and caprices of these arrogated leaders that have brought nothing new or creative to the populace. They need to be removed, sent packing with their old ways altogether. They have spent their own time. They have borrowed from the younger generation's time as well. And yet, they are ready to ride the future some more. They have stayed and overstayed.

The young politician made an impression on him and he volunteered to carry on the new crusade.

*****

THEY COME AND GO

When they come
We welcome them
with great ovation, éclat.
But when they go
Farewell!
we bade them,
with hisses.
They live an elegiac legacy,
For their generations
Whose mould has not been made
Into the Eldorado
Of oozing flints;
But that they have formed an echelon
Guarding the source they have destroyed.
They come with great fey,
Promising that they
Are not free fighters,
But rather free masons,
Come to Messiah the die-hards.
But they go living a turbulence
And weal-ful immemorial
Fat but dead purse,
Behind a joyfully blank hope
For tomorrow…
Nevertheless,
their styles
And chancery
will remain applauded,
hissful Model
Still they leave through generations
Unborn.

The drive to the office this morning was unusually smooth. The roads were free from all hiccups. The industrial action embarked upon by the workers to press home their demands for an increase in salary stirred. There was even a mutiny within the police – the law enforcer.

He has to go to work because he belonged to the high cadre: that class of people who will feel the hammer of the wrath of government should they decide to lay the striking workers off for being confrontational in the agitation for their rights. The whole economy has been ran aground by the never ending industrial action of the workers, paralyzing all economic activities, making the boisterousness of the city deathly calm and leaving the citizens to suffer for it. Sometimes, the workers have their demands met half-way or a quarter-way, but mostly they were forced to go back to work through government threats to sack any worker that failed to yield to the order of *get back to work*.

Many fifth-columnists amongst the union members leading the call for workers to give up on their collective bargain, claiming it is best to work and earn a little pay rather than stay at home and earn nothing at all. This was the only fall out of the union and the politicians fed fat on this weak link. Other than this, the union has been Marxist in their struggle which often times led to little or no achievement. Because as long as there is a society, there will always be divisions. The rulers and the ruled. The elite and the poor. Bourgeoisie and the pariah.

The strike action entered its second week even though there have been many truce meetings but all of them have ended in deadlock. The government has not shown its mighty power through the issuance of the return-to-work-tomorrow-or lose-your-job-circular this time, primarily because it was an election year and, typical of politicians, the party in power sought re-election. The leadership of the union saw this as an opportunity to push their demand for pay increase. The union invited her members to a meeting, begging all and making them know that this is a fight- to- win battle, because of the sensitivity of the era that they were. And they did won. The government announced a thirty percent pay increase. Although it was far below their initial seventy percent demand, it still was joyful news. Good that they had something plumping up their salary.

The household items have increased in price and tremendously reduced in quantity and quality. Water. Electricity. Gas. Waste disposals. Cable TV. Not a single bill was spared the inflationary hammer.

He's so happy to hear the announcement in the news. Not the pay rise really, but that he would be leaving home in the morning and returning in the late hours again. It was soothing. For he was anything but comfortable, being forced to stay back at home with his wife and kids. When he tried leaving home the third day of the strike action his wife stalked him by standing at the doorstep. She was prepared for that moment. She stood statue-still at his attempted exit from the room. He was aware of the show and so he abided by the rule. The rule of sit-at-home. Besides, there was no work in the real sense of it.

The last fight they had came to his mind. One of their rumbles. A sizeable audience has gathered in the name of being peace makers to witness a ring-less Wrestle Mania session. They fought one another shamelessly as they tore at each other with bites to bits.

The fight came about because the children were sent home from school due to non-payment of their fees. He wouldn't want the kids out of school but the delay in payment of his salary inadvertently led to so many bills piling up and unattended to. The children have been asked to come to school only if they can pay their fees. If they show up without the required money, punishment was to be lavishly given according to the Proprietor. The kids relayed the message to their mother as they did not want to be beaten. The mother waited for the father to come home at his usual late hour but when he did, he just shrugged her aside. The morning after, when she approached him, he complained that he was running late to work and he has some unfinished tasks from the previous day. The woman acted to enforce his paying of the children's school bills. It was better to confront him with the issues now, and if that meant stalking him, so be it. She decided to block him and have him listen to the issue there and then. Immediately, as he saw this, he flared into a tantrum complaining that his wife wanted him to lose his job. Arguments and counter-arguments; degenerate cacophonies awaken the children who were sleeping on the couch and the floor, to see their parents locked one into the other in what could best be described as a horn lock.

*****

The central counting system and *e*-voting option would be introduced in the coming election. This generated a lot of discourse amongst politicians, non-politicians, aligned and non-aligned political animals as well.

As long as people do not choose to be hermits, those people shall consciously or unconsciously drift towards politics either by expressing views parallel to the government's policies or by taking actions to install a better government.

The *e*-registration system has met with resistance as so many people feel disenfranchised via the new system, in a society where *e*-education was at a rock bottom level. The paper registration would have been more favorable because the people were familiar with that, and if there was at all going to be an introduction of any other system, it has to be gradual and not an instantaneous thing as being done. The non-educated and the partially-educated were the greatest in the populace and they saw anything *e*-compliant as a threat to their abilities and they deemed it an election for the elites alone.

The so called elites, who were far fewer in number than the less- educated, also saw this as an effort by the ruling party to pull the wool over the eyes of everyone in order to ensure their continued stay in office. Everyone condemned the *e*-system of voting outright. Because of so much rancor, the issue has created recess upon recess; even more so than was the usual character of the Senate. The minority leader has been crying foul since the announcement of the process. His party has been threatened to boycott the election if the electoral body goes ahead with the system, for they said it was all to the advantage of the ruling party.

On the morning of the announcement, the Chairman of the electoral body stated categorically that the new system will make things easier and the problem of double-balloting or double-counting will be eliminated. But the people knew too well that all that was mere hopeful speculation, based on the smooth flow of vote transfer to a central unit for counting, especially when the districts were numbering over a thousand, with additional numbers in thirty state divisions.

Surely, there must be more to this than meets the eye. A vote cast in a street within the district, of a state, could either get lost in transit to the central counting unit or get subtracted from the existing number of the opposition party. Better yet, a vote could be multiplied at three places if the vote is in favor of the ruling party. The ruling party calls the shots.

Though a Federal system, the President functions as all powerful Unitary Head. The central government is so powerful that if the President decides to mandate a state under him, no one will question him, as was evident when the allocation accruing to an opposition state was seized by the federal government for creating Local Council Development Areas. There have even been unprecedented situations where the President had gone into the Federation Account without consultation with his executive team or the Legislature approval for fund withdrawal, and given it to the electoral chairman to go purchase all the gadgets that would be needed, despite pending court cases potentially countermanding that very act. He was the father of the nation and he acted polymathily. Clear case of contempt of court but the President has immunity.

The Riot Act was read on national TV by the President. And what he read was an act signaling that whoever wished to go against the law of the land will be brought to book no matter how highly placed. The election must go on no matter who chose to boycott.

But, more often than not, the President's discretion superseded the constitution instead of the reverse. And he swore to protect the constitution with his life, without fear in the execution of his duties, nor to favor any individual, tribe, or clan. He has never been fearful in that execution of his duties, for he usually wielded the strong arm of the law against anyone who goes against the rules, often his rules, and gave great favor to any and all who pegged their political tent alongside his: The Untouchables.

One politician even boasted of the President's favoritism towards him while ensconced inside one of his swank guest houses with nubile girls his daughter's age, surrounding him. "We don't need to do much work as we are the ones to count the votes and read out the results. We only write our names on the log as the winning party in all of the districts of any state. And they are those that we have interests in. We do it with no hassles."

The people's votes count, but towards what? Not legitimate change or successful resolution of genuine problems. No.

The constitution allows for two terms of four years each. There were debates on how that section could be rewritten to allow for multiple terms by the incumbency. But, fortunately, it all ended as mere discourse with no hope of reality. So, all incumbent officers must follow the tradition, as members of the ruling clique will not open the files revealing any expenses while in office. And all officers seeking re-election must use all resources at their disposal to ensure their continued stay in office.

The elections had come to an end. Elections where there were champions and winners. The winners won the results while the champions won the votes and wrestled the results to the ground. The young politician that he met the other day was in the latter. Everybody in the district casted their votes for him but all of it went amiss in transit to the collation centre.

It was the kind of election where international observers reported to their media that it was a free and fair process. But the insiders knew that every sense of the democratic process has been totally stripped off. How can there be a sense of rule of law when the opposition has been totally gagged through the state apparatus, the police most especially?

The Commander-in-Chief ordered the state law enforcement agencies to ensure that no other people, except the members of the ruling party be allowed to freely sell their manifestos to the public. The Central decided who smiles and who cries, who goes, who stays, who lives and who dies. A man who has all the power of all the three arms fused in himself all alone.

Some voters were just all about immediate gratification hence they were easily bought with a cheaply peanut and sheepishly they trooped out to cast their destinies into the baskets of some scum.

Two months after the elections, the people still felt aggrieved by the imposition of leadership that they never desired but life moved on because everyone has been socially emasculated. If two people should meet to greet one another for a time longer than five minutes they might be charged with conspiracy against the government. Later, it may lead to treason which would land them behind bars and, if care is not taken, they might very well find their neck stretched at the end of a rope. Kids were kept under the watchful eyes of their parents and of law enforcement. Their parents watched them so that they wouldn't socialize too much. Nobody knew if teenagers will convince one another to take to the rhetoric of the terrorist. And from the rhetoric, it was a small leap to taking the actions of those scurrilous groups. Also, if teenagers will be quickly maligned as compatriots in the war on terror, out of a presumption of their naïve tendency to flock to rebellious associations and actions.

"Just come straight to the house when you close from school." Many parents would tell their wards repeatedly.

These words evoke some fear in the wards especially when gingered with some others, like, "The man in uniform may get hold of you if you wander about."

Everyone watched the public execution of some felons and no child would want to end up like that. To them, those people were villains.

There have been many Election Tribunals but nothing good was expected to come out of those sittings, as the same set of people comprised both the past and present sittings. Immediately, the general elections were over, election tribunals were set up and they continued sitting for well over four years. If there was going to be justice at all, it has long been delayed and probably denied. The status quo remains the status quo. No one bothered to file a petition.

It was an election for the highly hopeful. The impatient ones were long ago worn out by the never ending lack of productivity of the process. No equity anywhere you turn.

*****

As he sat in his office looking at the scar on his right hand; an after-effect of a first degree burn that he sustained while working in a confectionery store when he was trying to save up some money to further his education.

He was ordered by his superior in the kitchen section to light the cooker. Unbeknownst to him, the gas cylinder had been changed and the diffusing knob was left open with the invisible gas filling the room but the air was covered with the aroma of the pastries. He came in, jumping at the instructions of his superior, took the matchbox from the corner of the window where it was normally kept and he struck a stick.

He was jerked to life from his reminiscence, which had taken him ten years back, by his colleague coming in to use his staple machine.

"This is a scar I will never forget till death. How can I forget?"

That fire was quickly contained by the other staff and some customers present that day. He was given first aid treatment and allowed to go home to take proper care of himself. It took good seven weeks for the full healing to occur. He used petroleum jelly, not knowing that open air was the best approach to burn-healing. During this time, no member of the management of the confectionery store contacted him in any way, not to talk of a visit. He wondered why.

He went back to the office by the eighth week only to be informed that they didn't need his services any more. Fired! Donald Trump could not have announced it better.

His spirit was considerably dampened. His hopes of saving up for his education mostly crushed. He left a broken man.

*****

Everyone has their obsession. To some, it is their shirts and pants; this points to an obsession with their physical looks. Some cherish their books more than anything else that the world could offer. The inestimable value to others could be a strong faith in their religious beliefs, making them resign themselves to the fate of accepting anything as long as they see it as the will of God, good or bad. The ecstasy of having one's family around playing together at all times brings a very steady happiness to some, while the joy of having some other men keep one's company and deriving outlandish pleasure from that could be the greatest joy for some. Maybe it is the happenings in football, where a showdown between certain teams could be one of those great delights. But in all, I have come to understand that a man's delights changes as he evolves and advances in age.

In his teens, he had dreamt of becoming a Rabbi, seeing the lofty ways they get treated. The Rabbis do not hold their own books even while reading, not to mention having to heat their bath by themselves. There is always someone attending to them at one point or another. So, he dedicated much of his time to studying from the Torah to John The Beloved's discoveries of the life here after; that being the judgment to come on every birthed fetus and those that were accidentally or intentionally stopped from living life. His chance to wear the garments of the Rabbi was stalled when he walked into a room and saw a male neighbor holding one of their female neighbors tightly to himself in the course of their rough play. He had read somewhere that the eyes of a Rabbi should not see things like that. So, he bailed from that preoccupation.

At another time he wanted to pursue a career in law. He had the entire collections of Xerox copies of law journals and followed through on every development in the judiciary. It was quite an ambitious endeavor. But his dream was cut short when he was told that his family was too poor to sustain him through that course. Again, he detoured.

So many life changes impacted him over the years. And now, he was the sole provider for the household. His wife stopped working when her boss sexually harassed her.

She had been asked to wait for a brief discussion by that salacious boss of hers. The boss quickly walked to the door, bolted it to prevent anyone from bursting in.

"My sweet lady, you must have noticed that I have been ogling you for some time now and I have been looking for a way to be alone with you. Now I have the opportunity." What an automatic mentality of inappropriate entitlement that was!

He said all these words without any care regarding or respecting the matrimony of the woman. A married woman with kids! He walked to her back and held her shoulders gently as he worked his right hand across her bosom and cupped her left breast in his hand. She quickly sprang up from her seat, gave him the slap that he justly deserved, and walked out. So ended her brief career at that manufacturing firm.

In saner climes, the reckless approach by her boss would have been roundly dealt with and he would quickly have been jailed. Not here, though.

"It is better to keep my pride as a woman, intact, rather than submitting as a whore and opening my legs to any man other than my husband." That, she told proudly to a friend.

It has been months since she became a sit-at-home wife, for she has not been able to find another job. Most of the interviews she attended thereafter ended with one gratification or the other being demanded. What professional debauchery was this? Staying at home was preferable!

*****

As he drove home, after leaving the boys at their usual hang out, he thought about his family and the kind of beautiful life he would have loved to give them. The hopes that there were still better days ahead if he gets promoted were waning. Even to get promotion in the civil service you must find a professional mentor or godfather who must be willing to assist within the ranks. Or you have to belong to a club. Belong. And since he belonged to the Generation X elites, he has to forfeit his fast rise to the rules of professional initiation and membership. So, he continued with his quiet life, working hard as a camel but moving at snail's pace. Ahead of him, he met a roadblock with a policeman flashing him by some powerful flashlight; it was an indication to drive slowly and come to a halt at the roadblock. The primary security and law enforcement duties of the police have seen an added one; forced collection of dues from motorists was primary. This new maneuver to secure more money lands especially hard on the commercial truckers and those just wandering through.

He came to a halt at the checkpoint. He overheard one of the officers talking to someone on the phone and the impression was that the receiver must have been a woman of the street. Two other policemen approached him brandishing their guns. Old. Rusty. Dirty. AK 47 guns that may not even scare a bird. But the policemen brandished them anyway. The guys were in readiness to pull the trigger should there be any move to escape by any motorist. They reeked of so much alcohol that one would have thought that there might be a pool of alcohol somewhere around. Or, the metallic crest on their chests has just been polished with some ethanol. He grinned silently.

"Inner light!" They yelled.

He was amused but not surprised to hear the same command being yelled at a tricycle rider, even at times in broad day light. "Show your particulars," was the next command given.

Tonight, the policemen showed some sense of civility by playing down their earlier brutish approach. Voluntarily? Of course not. It was only because they had been under public scrutiny and then strong castigation for their unruliness regarding civil management. The force decided to do a general overhauling of its system by training its men. Mostly, the rank and file cadre. There were cases of trigger-happy officers which have led to the death of many people. In recent months, not less than five people have been felled by the bizarre actions of the police officers. One death involved a boy of twelve years old returning from school. There was no path to punishment for the police offenders which were spelled out. Immediately, when such happened, the officers quickly jumped into their vans and took off. Then a memo would be issued from the force headquarters saying that anyone who knew the officer who pulled the trigger should come to testify. And, of course, since the people knew that if they go for such a purpose, they will end up in a police cell or possibly being accused of being the killer. Everyone was cautious.

Wives beg their husbands, husbands beg their wives, and relatives beg one another to be cautious as to how they deal with these men-in-black, with obviously black character, for sure. Better still, stay away from them!

The words used in demanding the vehicle papers have shown that the new training was beginning to be rub off on them. Their interactions with drivers were more muted, tamed, and respectful. Inner Light. Show your particulars. A product of the smoother English for Specific Purpose.

He opened his pigeonhole and brought out the car papers as requested. The police officers scanned them and he got more amused to see the officers checking the papers upside down. He wondered if they know what they were looking at or even if they were able to read at all. Maybe too drunk.

"Na government car. Move along." That was determined after the officer shone his torch at the number plate of the car, not from the papers he held. "We are one and the same. No vex brother." They apologized.

His papers were given back to him pronto but they did not allow him to move. He, being a very good student of sign language, knew what they were saying and he parted with some notes. Oh, the omnipresent system of bribery in process. Yet, he was fortunate it was not thus high a price as it would have been had he been an ordinary driver. Everyone pays.

"What a force to be proud of." He said to himself when he was finally allowed to go. He remembered the other day when he went to a police station to bail his brother-in-law.

This relation had gone to lodge a complaint of breaking and entry into his own apartment. The complainant was detained as the first suspect when he could not come up with the payment they demanded from him for them to investigate. And when bailer arrived, even he had to haggle it out with them. Once, when his friend who was close to the scene of a robbery contacted the Police to come and stop a robbery operation, they complained of having no fuel in their vans. The robbers had a hitch-free session of killing and raping. For three hours, not a single police officer came into sight. The most horrific three hours of some people's lives. Hours of eternal pain that could have been stopped were the police able to show up and botched that which caused unwanted pregnancies, eternal loss of life, wheals and mass devastation imposed by the robbers.

Robbers are mortals, just as the policemen; the general public as well. The robbers have superior ammunition over the police. One would wonder where they get their machines of slaughter from. The police have greater power than the people because they are backed by law to shoot on sight, anyone who might be considered to be an aberrant, in as much as the police would use their discretion. And how much is that? The public is at the mercy of both the robbers and the police. And sometimes, it is difficult to tell the difference between the two.

He loved to editorialize as he was thinking. It satisfied some urge for decency within him.

*****

The women's gathering was fast growing into an association. It was the coming together of women in the neighborhood who were sit-at-home mothers.

"My husband is very loving. He brings me red roses every night." One of them talked amidst laughter of satisfaction.

Another told her story of rancor. Every day, her hope was to have a peaceful home. In addition, she wanted a loving husband and lovely kids. But her story was far from that. This much was obvious from the two deep, black depressions beneath her eyes; a sleepless woman. She got pitied by the other women, who consoled her of better things to come. One of them suggested a barbiturate.

"Is it now that he has risen to the top echelon of the company that he does not have time to come home again? Not to mention that he is rarely intimate with me." Another woman complained about her husband.

"Most men get busier as their business grows for it is much easier to start a business than it is to sustain it. Likewise, most men get merrier as their enterprise grows", a more matured woman had counseled.

"I remember when he was a junior staff. He would rush home at the close of work. Then he would stay indoors with me and we really enjoyed countless beautiful intimate sessions. I believe that was when he should have been busier. Not now that he has risen to the top", the woman insisted.

Truly, her husband was so busy lately. Rarely, did he go home. And when he did, he would be so tired. Very, very tired. Worn out by women who attended at his every side also. God save our men.

"If any man tries to be smart with me. I know how to pin him down." Another woman dropped with much ease.

No doubt, she understood how to pin them down. She got the best set of Prophets, Imams, and

Dibias in town, whose specialties in the mixtures of love potions to be served with food or to be used in making incisions around the waist line causing any man that eats her food or sleeps with her to lose his senses and never leave her for any other woman in the world, was unparalleled. She has countless men who would answer her calls for money; they must work tirelessly and endlessly to provide for her. She has so many others on her slave list. Yet some on her eviction list.

May the good God save men from such women.

"My boss has been so vindictive lately." Another chipped in. "He said that I have been revealing too much", she added. Looking at her, one would conclude that a whorehouse was not far away. The boss warned her several times, since he wouldn't want his marriage to be in jeopardy due to the high temptation the defenceless dressing of the woman potends. She felt scorned by the warning as she saw herself as a belle at some court even at fifty two. Her bosom was tightly guarded, fully protruding. She was decked out in a bare bottom with many colorful stripes flowing from the edge of her waist. A five button shirt but only two of those buttons were locked in.

"I will show that man the stuff I am made of", she bluffed and it didn't work well with her boss. She was the coordinator of the emancipation group. Her breasts were dancing; emancipated too. What is sacredly meant for one's spouse should not be in question with the public. Certainly not!

*****

Political feuds have been built amongst and within political parties as another general elections approached. Talks, controversies, arguments. In all of these exchanges, one thing was damn sure: the Presidency favors the incumbent. The political princelings were at each other's throats. Equal to these clashes, there was the need to cover up the mess of deeds which must not be opened to the public. A Pandora's Box. Especially as regards the international community. And that was because the incumbent had done everything possible to earn the recognition of foreign allies. Even to the extent of seceding part of the country. This could have been an oil rich region given over to foreign capitalists operating their own companies to leach the oil from Nigerian ground.

The notion of the incumbent always succeeding must be repeated for emphasis as it is the truth.

*****

Another man narrated his own story about how he organized the résumé and other credentials which earned his wife a job at a bank. Not that he could not provide for his family since it was just the two of them for now, himself and his wife, since there was no child at home, they were both free to work outside of the home. He believed that getting her into a paid job will allow them to stand much stronger as a financial and professional pair. More so, the sit-at-home status of his wife required changing as that would boost his own pedigree amongst his peers and family. But little did he know that he was succeeding in giving his wife better leverage to play games with other men.

He later found out the truth. The wife managed many amorous affairs with the Head and the Assistant Head, equally sleeping with other men in the bank; and that included the customers. That pretty much guarantees that she brought in the deposit target laid upon her. Lay, lady, lay. One lay after another it was.

He had noticed a sudden change in his spouse as at many times she denied him intimacy on the grounds of being too tired from working all day: She was truly working all day servicing numerous clients and their needs. He also discovered so many text messages as well. Text messages he had sent to his wife were repackaged by her and sent to her lovers. Rude, explicit, scenes.

It was so much torture to go through these kinds of messages on one's wife's phone; heart-wrenching, mind-killing, and deadly. At this point, he broke down and wept. A man who felt severely stabbed.

He had fought his family and friends when they kicked against his engagement to her. Now that their predictions were changing into reality, he now understood their initial stance.

Family and friends are treasures that must be heeded and not be thrown away. They are often the shield in the turbulence of life.

One day, the lady had come home past midnight, giving the excuse that she has been attending the inner caucus meeting being held across the banking industry. In fact, she had a presentation the next day regarding that. And, believing that her credit was his credit, he had worked on the presentation for her all night while she went straight to bed, rejecting the food he had rushed home to prepare for her.

He had been bewildered to discover that she had unconsciously called another man's name at the crescendo of coming down from the hilltop he had taken her to while he was making love to her. She was just there, almost lifeless, like a piece of log, closing her eyes so tightly when he pointed out the name calling to her. The fire of the marriage was gone, blown out by an ignominious immoral wind.

Traitors are usually those people who give their words but turn their back and forget that they just spoke to someone. The credibility of a person lies in words proving to be consistent with their deeds. It is so simple.

He came back to the pub. The last time he visited was a fortnight prior to his wedding. He had rushed out amidst heated argument with his friends, that his marriage would be filled with uncertainties as they jokingly reminded him of the redlight zone where he met her. They further told him that for such a viper to change for the better, it would require nothing short of a miracle, as the venom of a serpent is so dangerous and lasting even after the superficial skin is shed. He broke the bottle of alcohol that he had been drinking in the heat of that argument and he vowed never to return to the boys again. He would miss nothing if they didn't appear on his wedding day. He stormed out. Now, he was the one appearing on their turf again.

He has good company seated close to him; a budding businessman whose wedding plans got called off because the bride-to-be discovered a greater treasure only after their traditional engagement ceremony. She discovered that there was a man with whom she would much rather love to spend the rest of her life. This new man worked in a bank and already had two kids from two different women before her which morally made them simpatico since she can't be faithful to a man. Her friends gave warning of an almost certain abuse in his rage at her as well as in his impatience with her immoral ways. But she felt he does not have any righteous room to call his own. Their best hope was that he will forgive her behavior only because he would desire that she raised his children. And, on top of that, which was the worst irony of all, he was as craven as she was.

How easy it is to forget our own faults!

The unfathomable twists and turns of the hallways of human behavior are enormous!

And so the man seated beside him was ready to move on, just as he was summoning all the courage he needed to face the future ahead of him.

*****

UNFAITHFULNESS

More pain than pleasure
Cupid hath brought me;
Lying on the couch,
Pondering about Juliet;
Same pain she shares I doubt
In company of other Romeo
She dwells
Roaming hand-in-hand
Along the archway
With man-Friday
Singing lullaby to him she does
At the night of night,
In him
She sleeps
I know not
but everyday
Killing myself
With pleasure of pondering
About her.

A lot has happened, during the above a decade, since the ruling party has been in power. Years fraught with dissatisfaction and silent protests, by both civil and uncouth societies, militant, and regional groups. Secession calls; balkanization along different divides of interest but with many hurdles as the mixture of black and white is fast flaring.

Come let us reason together. The call for secession should not be a singsong at all. To make it clearer, it should not be a part of our history in any way. What will happen to my sister who got married to a man from the East? What will be the fate of my cousins whose father is an Islamic cleric and mother an Evangelist? What damage do we bring to our national psyche when we separate our kids from playing with one another? The poles between us are just barriers that we have built through our geographical mappings, but our true identity runs in our veins as we are human beings living together, making attempts at cooperatively deriving the maximum benefits that life has to offer to all, and to witness the joy of great days ahead with a sense of assurance composed of the hopes for a better tomorrow.

And as one indivisible entity we will remain. That incorporates love, peace, and unity.

*****

There was a sickly President who left the reign of governance to his First Lady. He was not medically fit to serve. In fact, on occasions, when he was unable, Presidential orders were brought to the fore directly by her. Now I begin to understand the influence of the feminist thrall affecting the dominance of the egotistic male species. All men bow to her.

Many Presidential aides became sweepers and cooks with their gold crested cat suits. Compensations, contracts, deals, oil blocs. Daughters married to strategic men in the society. All were the creation of imperial wife of the number one citizen.

Appearing and disappearing acts became the state's tool to resuscitate the head whose nation knew nothing of his ailment. An ailment whose diagnosis is not known can never be treated.

There was a serious cabalistic power tussle between the powers that be; those in the feast and those that wanted to come on board. Continual grip onto power is a lifeline that any power drunk would not want to lose.

The Vice President man must be sworn in, since the constitutional provision stipulates that. There was a high tension between parties and their respective interests, but, ultimately, they must yield to the constitution. They held the country at bay for a while, but no longer as the providence following the number two citizen cannot be wished away. But providence is not just enough for leadership because it can only help one attains success: it can never help one to maintain such accidental success.

A new reign began. It was a government that thrived on lies; gross ingratiation at the expense of the masses. Massive corruption was attenuated to mere pilfering. They brazenly show feigned statistics that are far from the realities of the living conditions of the masses. They make piddling progress with a prodigious budget. How can an outsider tell you the interior of your house better than you know it yourself? The fish in my pot I know so well. So I needed no Fitch to tell me what I know. Victoria's secret is in the public glare.

A state madam with relatively overlord functions became a national burden to bear. Many of his aides and blind loyalists- vocal pyromaniacs- also became campaigners of all forms of squalidness. They were at work on many media platforms with overt subterfuge to water down the collective contriteness of the people, as most people were already biting their thumbs by allowing their sentiments to overrule sound objectivity in him voting during the last elections as he had come with the mien of a gentleman but time revealed his high disposition to monstrosity and his penchant for corruption. He was a chief crusader of everything putrescence; coupled with his gross incompetence and crass behavior both at the local and international levels.

Never trust a man who was bereft of a satiated upbringing with your commonwealth. Given opportunity, he will deplete it in a bid to compensate for his lost childhood and in fear that his misfortune may soon return as the door shuts at his departure. He will be so obstreperously accumulative of wealth even to his own self-destruction - *Omo-Aijoberi* syndrome.

Impugn Impunity.

There is no good leadership when that leadership is lacking a good head. People clamor for leaders that won't say "all these things did not start with my government"; someone that will take responsibility and act as a leader. Not some sufferer of intelligential myopism.

*****

They had been married for twelve years after being introduced by a mutual friend. Both were of legal maturity. They took their possibilities seriously. She was so desperate to be a married woman, at the least. She wanted so badly to be referred to as someone's wife. A Mrs. She had suffered much stigmatization for still being single at thirty nine. It was a well-attended wedding ceremony. And all the bills were solely paid by her. That was one of her greatest desires, to provide for him. She had always wanted a tall, rich, handsome man. Not much to ask for, she believed. She had to wait till age thirty nine so that she could sort and shuffle all of her candidates over time. Some other suitors she met were employed but didn't meet all other criteria on her list or that the kind of job that they possessed didn't really fit her choice, so she waited patiently until she came in contact with this sweet talker.

Of course he was handsome, muscular, oil dealer, all of the truly important qualities for a man in life.

They became live-in lovers almost immediately. After six months, they decided to make the relationship official. Even though many factors doomed this relationship of shallowness, she was so blind to it all. Truly, how does an oil dealer remain so broke? The excuse that she accepted was that he had invested so much in some vessels which were still on the high seas, or, on shore but not ready to be bled of its oil for use. And during those six months of excuses, he would come home with flashy cars, attend meetings, and come back home pretending to be busy writing business proposals.

"My ships will berth soon", he would say this amidst a thousand smiles.

The lady was so understanding, bankrolling his outings, hoping that she would get reimbursed when the ships' cargo were emptied. She was unable to understand that her money bought his flashy new cars, nothing else.

Desperation is a very costly emotion.

It was only after eleven years that she was able to realize her folly when snippets had it that the great gigolo was about to reenact his usual life with another. She started getting the news that he was father to eight other kids from four other women.

Being a law enforcer, great sleuthing followed. She got to the truth. About time! Her husband had been married to other women of different calibers. One of them was the company secretary to one of the popular multinationals. Another was the daughter of a telecommunications tycoon. In turn, they had conceived children for him and were all still married in a big ring around the rosy. Ashes, ashes, we all fall down!

Traditionally, polygamy was not an issue at all. But he had been married legally to these women within the provisions of the Marriage Act, which only recognizes one man to one woman. Not all women realize this right is given to them by the law as they strongly believe men would always be men and rut with abandon.

She presented him a parcel as a warm welcome, upon his return from one of his trips. He must have gone to see one of his families. She was extraordinary romantic that night. She was so agile that she wore him out after round upon round of sex.

Women could be very dangerous. She could have poisoned him had she wanted. To kill, though with the hiss of pleasure, provides a unique sweetness of its own in a situation like this.

He anticipated something gleaming and good within the parcel. He smiled with the foolhardiness of a man certain of his rights in spite of his outrageous behavior. But this parcel was a total deviation from the norm. About time again! He was faced with barrages of pictures of his different families, theirs included. He became visibly shaky, sweaty even. His pores gave up water-soaked stains to his shirt even, while the air conditioner was blowing at his fullest.

He lost all speech.

*****

Many youths were offered Presidential pardon, after many had committed atrocities in the fight for self-dependence and resource control, in the name of Amnesty. Their region suffered from degradation and deprivation. They have suffered economically and environmentally from oil exploration. There was so much community destruction through this process. The water was polluted, farmlands destroyed, and the sludge of oil was everywhere. The youths took to arms to resolve their own crises as they thrashed it out with various oil companies.

Ab initio. It was treated with kid gloves until it became a scourge. Truly, the course for rebellion was justified in the beginning until it became a livelihood for some lazy youths who wanted an easy stroll into wealth. They turned into felons. Oh, it became a national headache. The movement lost its purpose when inner division developed. The unified cause suddenly was composed of different ideologies and different groups. The unified cause was that of a righteous fight till the end; the end being the proper right of place and interests given to the host communities in their oil producing areas.

After much interference with the oil operations. Abduction and demand for ransoms became the norm then their regalia became ceremonial.

Necklaces bore ostentatiousness. Aberrations of a freedom-fighter in total. A dog chain. An insignia of perpetual mental imprisonment. Poverty of the highest order.

A right cause is right as long as it favors the majority of the populace for whom it is fought. Any movement loses its cause the day that it becomes monetized.

*****

In the court, one of the two judges was sweating profusely as he sat listening to the case of a man of God accused of obtaining money under false pretense. The gavel of authority looked weightier than his wrist. He looked unfed with his bespectacled owl eyes.

The supposed Pastor gave special spiritual baths to a phony politician and his family. He was protecting them against his dreaded political opponents. The politician came for cleansing and purification. He was tied in white raiment and kept in a barrel for hours; various candles of different colors burned to ward off evil. And it was also done to secure his election bid. Other concoctions and incisions followed. The wives and daughters also came for consultations. The wives were made to dance unclothed around an effigy, as he watched and later took them in for one-on-one consultation one after the other. They wanted a male child and that was what he was helping them out with. More manipulations made in the interest of conning the gullible.

So many people are shameless. Just as many politicians are. And many of these call themselves holy. Shakesparian, "the hood does not make the monk."

*****

Bombshells from the neighboring countries and the movement of the earth's crust coming from the blast of grenades were now common features of the sight and sound. The chants of imminent war in some sister countries included protests against a vitiating leadership, and a fight with the aim of effecting a change of that leadership has not being the true representation of popular sentiment.

The world is truly changing, not just politically but also climatically. For example, it has left so many seas to create algae blooms as a result of the punctured ozone layer. The many rippling side effects are tremors, earthquakes, and tsunamis. The psychology of many people has been so perverted that they launch different moves to overturn many ideologies. The seventeenth century's Knight Templars are being launched once more. They are just one of many established. Jihadists take this label too.

We should know that peaceful coexistence does not mean that we should obliterate some people or carry out a holocaust ever. That thinking is anathema. A splendid variation in life is vivid and required. To be mature is to accept the diversity rampant in nature: flora, fauna, and people, of course, of all colors, sects, and ideologies. I am certain so many social psychologists may not be able to define the impetus responsible for people to clothe themselves with bombs and detonate same in a bid to carry out an order. And lo, it is carried out with such certainty, the light of fanaticism in their eyes. A term, menticide cannot be ruled out. What a tragedy!

IF I SEE

If I see Osama
I will give him a hug
A handshake
Maybe that is what he needs
To know that there is beauty
In Humanity.

If I see Bin Laden
I will take him
Around the wonders
Of the world
To see the beautiful landscapes
And architectural masterpieces
Humans have made out of nature.

If I see the handsome man of Afghanistan
I will make him see babes
Playing joyfully in gardens
How beautiful it is to see them
Innocent faces. Pure hearts.
Racist-less. Bonding happily.

If I see Osama Bin Laden of Afghanistan
I will make him read Alfred Nobel's creed
The beauties of the world in living
Living positively
Making history, positively.

A WORLD

A world of war
Striving Success
Running Race
Motionless, Timeless
Tireless, Boundless,.
Friendly foes
Foeing friends
Captivated Liberty…

What a world

Beautiful Beasts

Handsome Hulks

Adieu Births

Glamorously Ridiculous

Refinedly Crude

Smoothly Rough…

A confine
Largely small
Penuriously Affluent
Strongly Fragile
Fatly Slim
Endless Stops…

A platform
Acrimoniously Quiet
Warring Peace
Overtly Covert
Absurdly Logical…

What a world
Wickedly Nice
Crystally Blurred
Alluring Tears…

A certain fifty seven year old man has just inherited his own stepbrothers as stepchildren following the demise of his father. His stepmother is now his wife. That is the tradition.

His legally married wife has kicked against this but she has no choice other than to bow to the dictates of the agelong tradition. They already have five children, consisting of three girls and two boys of marriageable age. In fact, two of the girls are married already. They all are stunned at this development. They had thought this particular tradition to be backward and, therefore, should no longer be practiced.

But just as some men like unique possibilities, so does he. He is so eager to obey the tradition. He is so ready to obey what the traditions have said. This tradition speaks to him joyfully. It is complex and arcane, but magnificent as well: his half- brothers are now his step sons, and are half-brothers to his children as well as to their uncles; step-sons to his wife; his step-mother is now his wife.

One wife by law, two wives by custom. It is a great complication to explain. Very knotty.
But that is the tradition. And sanctified traditions are always wise. Aren't they?

Very many modern scholars have been at the forefront of the crusade for the repeal of this tradition. But often times these arguments meet with strong brick walls, as many that were chosen to work on the revision of such tradition are the same people who have benefitted immensely, directly or indirectly, therefrom.

They see it as a way of keeping the family's appurtenances within the family. Many a time, the bequeathed challenges this tradition. Such rebellion is neutralized by removing that very person from the inheritance in question. And since these objectors, usually women of little means, throttle down or even turn off their objections entirely at the prospect of their loss of claim to an inheritance, nothing more need be said.

I wonder when the women will also inherit men; where a sister will inherit her deceased sister's husband so that she will have two husbands. After all, it is a tradition, a norm. They should equally enjoy the same benefit. The tradition requires application to all or it is nothing more than a biased passing of wealth to men only. So, if a tradition cannot or will not be applied impartially, gender fair in particular, remove it.

And what is that but sexism; and a dehumanizing, sordid process?

SOCIETAL FRAGMENTS

MAKING OFA
MISANDRIST

It's a rainy Saturday morning. She had run to her common haven, "my husband beat me all night!" she mentioned again in her usual cadence. Now and then, she runs like this to Iyabo's house.

Iyabo is her aunt; she is a very stoic lady with an English accent. It is a curious thing, her accent. She sounds as if she has lived in the arms of the United Kingdom forever when in actual fact she has only visited the country twice according to the information on her passport. And those two visits only lasted seventy two days the first time and ninety days the second. So how does she manage such a perfect accent?

The mind wanders on occasion. It is a sweet thing that the human mind does this.

"Can't this your husband stop being an animal that he is? I won't let him kill you while I am here. I think it is high time you packed your things and left him for good." She throws that in just for good measure.

On many occasions, Iyabo has gone to fight Dedapo in his wife's stead. The last time was about a fortnight ago when Dedapo accused Sayo of infidelity because she would not answer her calls in his presence. He beat her near to death and rushed her to the family hospital nearby. Regular visitors they have been, with records of wounds and injuries from domestic violence. On one particular occasion, Iyabo tore Dedapo to shreds with her finger nails. Guess what? Many patterns were also drawn on him with her enameled dentition.

One would have thought that would be the end of Sayo and Dedapo's cohabitation as they had only been a common law couple for the past eight years, off and on. But rather, Dedapo, in his usual way, bought some gifts and flowers and had them delivered to Sayo while she was still in the hospital with a note:

IN THE WHOLE WIDE WORLD,
THERE IS NOTHING MORE PRECIOUS TO
ME THAN YOU.

Hallmark couldn't have said it better.

A few minutes after her receipt of the gifts, he walks in, goes down on his knees, tears rolling down his cheeks, and says, "I don't know what usually come upon me. I just can't stand the idea that another man might be sharing you with me. I am sorry, Ololufe mi."

They both then burst into fiery tears for a few minutes and later on console one another. Sayo reaffirms her commitment to him and makes him know that there is no other man for her and she desires to walk home with her husband. Hand-in-hand, showing a perfect Romeo-and-Juliet-like love that a new neighbor might wonder what a perfect love Cupid has wrought, they leave the hospital. But soon enough, their conclusions are dashed and their only question is how Cupid's arrow could have become so bent so quickly.

Born Adedapo Jaiyesimi, into the royal Abegunde family of the Isiwo kingdom, now a project coordinator in a construction company and an alumnus of the prestigious Ile-Gogoro University, he is a polished, cute, young man. His future is highly promising; much above his peers for he is of high intelligence. His parents separated when he was barely two years old. He has only an elder sister. They must go with their mother. She would not ever leave them behind with their wino, lazy, serial divorced father.

According to the story told, their mother fell in love with their handsome father. He was a power dresser and spoke with flaming oratory. It started with a routine visit, followed with an adulation that yielded to every act of kindness as if being offered a seat, a seat taken. He promised her he would stop drinking once they got married; it was his loneliness, after all, that caused his drinking. It was the same lame excuse that many men would give and many women would take in naivety in utter desperation for marriage. Anuptaphobia!

She was in her late thirties and was already being pestered to bring her man home. She was not impressed by any other man and he had pressured her for a while now, so she deemed his presence and pressure gratifying. She gave in to him. His feeble backstory had been that he had once fallen in love with a certain lady, whom he sent to school. She graduated and then graduated from him. It was told in an unvarnished fashion, or so it seemed. It was actually one of those incredible stories that would surely attract a great level of sympathy, such that anyone might want to offer their own sister or daughter to him in marriage. Or, at the very least, shore up their assent and capitulate to all else.

By the tenth month, she invited him to meet her parents and they concluded there and then, almost as he stepped into their home, to come take his wife in a few weeks' time. There were no background checks as tradition demanded. They were in such a hurry to let her go because they saw it as tradition's disgrace for their daughter to remain unmarried till her late thirties while still living with them. This is the same tradition that demands background checks be done on any suitor but also condemns a woman to staying single till past her mid-twenties, what a tradition!

A bottle of dry gin is really all that it will take as a gift to accomplish the deed of marriage permission.

A few months after the wedding, all was rosy and loving; all involved were highly responsive and responsible. The first child came, Adedara, the perfect replica of her beautiful mother.

"I thought you said it was loneliness that makes you drink. Now you have me and your daughter. How is it loneliness now?" She asked him one night after he came home in his usual state of stupor.

He had stopped keeping late nights just as he had promised before their marriage but he could not stop drinking. It was a disease with no end that he suffered. Prior jobs of his were crushed by this infirmity.

One wonders how he is able to afford the drinks but no matter how much one tries to unravel this magic, there remains a mystery.

Stories started filtering in about his past marriages. They had all collapsed because nothing could really separate him from the love of his beer. In all of it, he was never a violent man, but disgraceful; to himself and family. Many times he laid in road beds, gutters, and unlikely places for human beings with their rightful senses to find themselves in. Those rightful senses abandoned him long ago in the ongoing current and tide of alcohol.

The wife endured. Persevered, Believed. Hoped for a change; hopelessly really as none came. Then in time, the second child came, Adedapo, a look-alike of his father.

The father degenerated further. He started selling household items, though he was not the one who bought them, to pay off his many debts at different beer parlors. He even went to the point of selling their mattress. How he got to this point, no one quite knew, though all had their urgent guesses. He came from a religious lineage. But they knew that religious beliefs played no part in it; the gin sucked his right senses up until they were dry as a bone and he had none remaining.

In one of his sober days, he had told his wife how his own father called all of his children together one day and told them, "I know I am in my twilight."He was in his eighties."I may be visited by some sickness and you may think I am gone. Do not bury me until you have dropped some sips of gin in my mouth. If I drink it up, that means I am still alive and my heart is beating, but if not, then I am gone." The children laughed over it but they observed the rite for the old man anytime he seemed to slow until he finally passed at the age of one hundred and one. Alcohol never affected the number of years that he grew to.

When Adedapo heard this story about his paternal relations, he told himself he would not take to drinking. His mother did her best to raise them, him and his sister with Christian values. She single handedly raised them, educated them, and nurtured them to the best of her abilities. He cut off any tie with his paternal relations. That was easy as none of those people cared to seek his mother, sister, or himself out ever.

Iyabo is the only family relation that Sayo has. She is her paternal aunt who has taken care of her since her mother abandoned her eight months after her birth.

She was born Adesayo Iretiola Campbell, a descendant of Olowogbowo, of Brazillian Quarters in Lagos Island, A well-trained and seasoned banker, and an alumnus of Lagos Business School; a rising star in the banking industry. Very pretty, average height, with an elegantly glowing skin of an Amazon per excellence. At times, one would wonder if her rapid rise in the banking industry is based on her physique, for no single eye will behold such a beauty and not willingly go out to offer a hand of favor even when it is not solicited. But in the real sense, Sayo is a very responsible and sensible lady. A lady ready to put aside all toga of aristocracy. She is ready to rise to the topmost ladder of her chosen career through hard work: a professional par excellence.

Her mother, who was a highly placed woman in business circles, did not want to have anything disturb her business and political engagements. She was the Permanent Head of the government delegation to the conference for Women in Power, otherwise known as WIP, being held in Geneva annually.

Her father was a diplomat in one of the high commissions. One might have mistaken him for a non-African because of his skin color and his name, Dacosta Oladepo Campbell.

Madam Igbayilola, Sayo's biological mother, had been married twice. In fact, she was still married to her second husband with two children from that marriage. She met Dacosta in one of those numerous conferences of hers and they grew impassioned with one another. Of course, it ended in their sleeping together for the two-week duration of the conference.

A conference without perks is no conference at all.

Truly, no woman who saw Dacosta, if not strong, was able to resist his gentlemanliness and handsome looks. And no man was able to resist Igbayilola with her heavy bosom and figure eight bodily structure.

What was to be a fling became an issue that none of them wanted. Abortion was way out of consideration for her because she was too old for the risk of it and there was nowhere she could go where they would not ask for her identity. More so, Dacosta wanted the child so badly because his marriage to the Rwandan was barren. She had lost her womb having been repeatedly and savagely raped in a war that rocked her country some years back. What a dilemma?

His marriage to the Rwandan subsisted and he wanted a child. Igbayilola's marriage too subsisted and she did not want the child due to the pregnant possibilities of scandal back home.
Oh, the permutations of possibilities with the ramifications when driven by potential scandal. Scandal, just like an onion, once peeled, insistently and endlessly sheds its smell deeper and deeper, stronger and stronger.

They devised a way out. Her schedule allowed her to stay out of her home for a long time. She could carry the pregnancy in a foreign land and then, at the last moment, have it delivered and deposited with his sister back home, Sayo's Aunt Iyabo. The sister would take over from there. In that time, Igbayilola managed to go back home in shape. Once that was accomplished, she then moved on. She agreed to that especially with the huge benefits that came with it.

Igbayilola had been a very cunning woman, ready to do anything, name it, anything, to remain in the social and political circles. Her first marriage crashed when it was discovered that she was pregnant while her husband was medically confirmed to be sterile. Not every man would accept a Jesus-like birth. Immaculate conception just was not the norm, was it? She had to move out of the man's house and she lost the pregnancy due to the stress of the scandal. To the present, she never divulged who was responsible for the pregnancy. She was so good at keeping secrets secret. Her skills were vast.

Dacosta only kept in touch with his daughter through his sister. He only came face-to-face with her just a few times since her birth when he strode into town for meetings. He never tried to take her out of the country on his own alone for he knew the Rwandan woman, his wife, might catch wind of that information and that might lead to exactly what he was trying to avoid; scandal. But he never starved Sayo and Iyabo of funds. How admirable was that?

The more reason Sayo was able to attend the best university in Nigeria.

Igbayilola, since the delivery, never bothered to discover the whereabouts of the child.

Anyway, part of the terms stated that she must steer clear of her child anyhow. In her mind, she was only adhering to the contract terms. Indeed, she was being a good player.

God would be well pleased with that.

And Sayo would never know her true mother.

"I see no sense in what you are doing." Iyabo had shouted.

This was in a bid to stop Sayo from moving in with Dedapo initially but Sayo would not budge. She was madly in love. Love is like that; an addiction without reason. The same goes for someone hooked on drugs. That euphoric delusion has such a kick. No matter what you do to stop the urge, there is no budging until peril looms and can no longer be denied or ignored.

"I will have to call your father at this point." Iyabo threatened.

She came calm at the mention of her father because they had not bonded at all. How could bonding take place over the phone or with teleconferencing? All she felt about her father was that of the constant flow of cash. That was all.
Iyabo tried to stop her by any means necessary from moving in with Dedapo, even when she had to phone Dacosta to inform him of the situation.

"She is old enough to determine her own choices." Dacosta had said this over the mouthpiece of the phone after being briefed by Iyabo about the case. Iyabo felt so deflated but not disappointed as she knew her brother to be a totally liberal person when it came to certain issues, maybe a little inhumanly indifferent at times too.

Sayo was twenty three and already working and earning her own living.

Iyabo feels defeated the next day after Sayo's departure and becomes so lonely. All alone in the expanse of her living room, she watches her favorite movie. It is *Sarafina*. She had seen the movie over and again because it helped teach her the true essence of self-determination and personal fight for freedom.

Born Iyabo Segilola Campbell, she is the third child and the second daughter of the family. Dacosta still is the only son. Their eldest sister died years ago in a hit and run accident. It was a gory sight that the family did not want to remember.

Iyabo and Dacosta grew up together, loving one another as a sister would love her brother and vice versa.

Their father, Chief Augustus Oladehinde Campbell, a palm oil merchant was in his early sixties then. He was forthright, liberal, and adroit, such that his foreign partners took extra-ordinary interest in him. Many favors were done for him; the most significant of which was guiding his son to a scholarship into Cambridge. Their mother, Oluwanisola Aduke Campbell, assisted her husband in his trade. She was a devoted Christian and a well-cultured woman of great influence amongst the local women in her church and environment. She was either at the store with her husband or home attending to her children.

She told the children how she was betrothed to her husband from birth by her parents who happened to be family friends to the senior Campbells. That was the custom popular in their own time. So both of them grew up to accept one another as man and wife; predetermined by their own parents.

Iyabo and Dacosta communicated through letters and telegrams. It was even Iyabo that would take notes from her parents and have them sent to her brother via the post or emissaries.

Iyabo attended the best fashion school in town as she made it known to her parents that she would not want to waste her time studying what she didn't have any flair for. So, she chose fashion, typical of the Western mentality; and because Dacosta had grown into it himself, he gave his nod. His nod was critical as his opinion must be sought in this matter affecting the future of his esteemed sister.

While at fashion school, Iyabo met a handsome young man of about the same age and they kicked it off there and then. They were so in love that they were determined to get married. They were not sleeping together; moral grounds compelled these two Christians to consider sex done outside of the circle of marriage as adultery and a great sin before the eyes of God.

"I am sorry, Iyabo!" The young lad startled as he reeled out his lines. "I will not be seeing you again!" Tears rolled down his cheeks.

"Why?" Iyabo had asked simply.

"My parents have promised me to a certain family friend's daughter and I must obey their wish." He had finally submitted to tradition and his parents.

They both broke down and wept endlessly. That was all that they could do. And cry they did.

One would wonder what kind of tradition it is that hands out a man to a woman and vice versa without the consent of the parties in all of the arrangements. Weird that one might have to submit to something that is outdated and should have been long discarded.

She locked herself up in her room. The feeling of loss, of love lost, especially to her, felt overwhelming. After months of hiding, she bounced back to life, resumed her fashion school classes and met with friends again. She was joined onto life once more. But this time, concentrating on fashion, she had no spare time for anything else. Her motto:

NO FRIVOLITIES.

A year passed and most of her friends were already engaged, some were even married or planned to get married. And many times, she had been pressured by her friends to meet some of their lovers' friends, but she refused vehemently. As time passed though, she gave in. Bodunde was the man who caught her fancy.

Bodunde was a handsome, working class guy who lived on the Victoria Island. He was bespectacled with a nerdish appearance that suggested the mindset of a bookworm. He was more advanced in age than her. Again, she started to get her groove back.

One evening, on their way home from an outing, Bodunde, drunk and in the company of his other friends, was involved in an accident that killed him and two other occupants of the car.

It was reported that they ran under a parked trailer at about 2AM. They would have survived had rescue come in good time: he died due to blood loss while he was trapped in the vehicle stuck under the trailer. His body gave it up before they could be taken to the hospital at about 5AM. In fact, one of the legs of the only surviving victim had to be amputated. He alone lived to tell the story.

Iyabo mourned Bodunde for another long period. This time, her parents had been worried about her sanity as she seemed to have snapped immediately after the shocking news of Bodunde's death was broken to her. But it took only a few weeks for her to return to normalcy this time. She had gone back into her shell. But Dacosta came to visit during this period and offered this twenty year old woman his shoulder to lean on. This was a true brother. They were so close. They understood one another so perfectly, even from a distance. They communicated so well. Telepathic mates almost. He offered to take her with him but their parents refused on the grounds that no one would take care of them if both of their children left.

Dacosta had been married to the Rwandan at this time. This suffering wife of his was suffering not at his hands, but rather those of a pack of vicious Rwandan rebels who had captured her temporarily. She had righteously and rightfully refused to set her foot on African soil again after her escape. These same rebels nearly eliminated her entire family as well. Her fears were justified. She had been savagely raped round after round by one rebel after another. She was feasted upon by these supposed champions of change and a more righteous way of life. Since her escape from their grip, and after being granted asylum in the United Kingdom, she never came back to Africa. She only sent her greetings to her in-laws through her husband. She suffered grave nightmares each time the scene of the livid inferno that nearly consumed her family came to her mind.

Iyabo picked the pieces of her life up and attempted to put them back together as she ventured into her own fashion business. She started off in one of her father's shops within her parent's house in the Isale Eko area.

It was one of those evenings when Isale Eko was bursting with so much activity that this particular young man walked into Iyabo's shop and demanded that a special native dress be made for him. The design was only one of his goals buried in his request. This he made known eventually, when he asked the lady who stood up to attend to him, taking Iyabo to be an attendant or an apprentice in this big shop.

"Where is your Madam?" His ulterior motive was exposed.

Iyabo feigned ignorance and responded, "my madam is not around. How may I help?" She was not sure why she had done this exactly. Instinct came to her mind.

He must have come, just like many of them had done in the past, on a tip that a single lady from a wealthy family operated that big shop, hoping of course, that they could court her and then go straight into the family's wealth. She wondered how many guys thought this way, handsome. lazy, gold diggers, fortune scavengers, opulence freaks.

No one would take Iyabo as the proprietor because she chose not to adorn herself with gold, typical of an Isale Eko lady that owns such a magnificent shop. She couldn't be the owner as so many men and even women passed her by, probing deeper into the shop, seeking the real madam of the place. She was always dressed simply but elegantly; only for those who had the eyes to appreciate what class without excess adornment really meant. She knew how not to fall for superficial falsity.

Her father's last wish was for her to get married as soon as possible as the old man had ripened in age and was ready to ascend to the great beyond at ninety six. He passed on in the arms of his son. It had always been Dacosta's wish that his father die in his arms rather than be called upon to come pack the corpse of the old man. His father, Chief Oladehinde Campbell prayed for both of his children and just as they were singing his favorite song, *Amazing Grace*, he passed on to glory. What a magnificent way to yield up to the ghost!

A befitting funeral was performed as was due a great man who had touched many lives. Every family and friend, and there were many, went back to contemplate once the service was over. Iyabo was left alone to reminisce upon her life. So many pains endured and still single at thirty one. Why was marriage so on everyone's mind?

Singleness for a lifetime might serve the particular individual well. Could the culture not see that? It must be blind.

She became apprehensive. Would she ever get married? Especially, when she had to do all the things to grant her old father's dying wish. A desperate thought flashed through her mind. She had read about tricks that many women had to employ in a bid to get a man hooked. Many unspeakable things:

ONLY SMART GIRLS GET MARRIED

She laughed at some of the suggestions some supposedly smart girls had suggested to her.

-   GET PREGNANT FOR HIM.
-   BE AGRESSIVELY LOVING ALL OVER HIM.
-   INCENTIVES.
-   COOK HIM INTO SUBMISSION.

Iyabo is a sensible lady. She reads between the lines of their suggestions but in all, she perceived great doom at the end of each one. How could one get pregnant for a man that might not be willing to be a father to that child? And if marriage miraculously happened anyhow, the man might one day decide to walk away on the grounds that he was trapped via the child from the pregnancy.

Another one was being overtly all over him. That suggested a knack for fakery. When one was not actually in love, but was pretending to be , it would inadvertently lead to great peril. For what one might gain would all end like a flash in the pan. Gone. Abruptly.

And if one were employing incentives to get a man, to convince him of marriage's sweetness, her bill- paying promises, gifting, or other material shams would invariably draw not a man but a greedy, materialistic male. The difference between a man and a male is that the former has to do with sensibility while the latter is just about physique and superficiality, which will eventually lead to the male chauvinist's exit when such incentives cease to flow as expected.

If you cook him into submission, then you have to be ready to learn new cuisines every now and then in order to keep such a man at home. If not, he will go elsewhere where the food is seemingly tastier.

All the suggestions were devious and have lost all potency for that reason. Real love was what was required for her. She knew it. For better, for worse. She made up her mind! Her love would not be bought or sold with gifts, money, dinner, or even sex. It was only available to a man that would know her intrinsic worth and be ready to stake it all on that will win her over. She called their suggestions:

DESPERATION VIRTUES

She recalls a drama she had seen sometime ago.

WOLFSHEEP

OMNI: Bro Bolaji, a well-dressed, handsome young man, vibrant with massive energy; sharp and well-spoken in addition.

BOLAJI: *(Soliloquizing)* This morning mass is
            productive o. Thank goodness, I was able
            to talk to that pretty sister. *Ab initio*, she
            was doing yanga for me but who can resist
            me? Me *(Self adulation)* Finest Boy! *(Smiles)*
            What time is it? *(Checks his wrist watch.)* It is
            just a few minutes to nine. Yes! I can still
            make it to the service of that other church.
            Let me rush. I will catch some babes.
            Check out my Luigi pair of trousers and
            Lois Vuitton belt. Altogether, I am
            designer's dream. *(Rushes out.)*

Scene II

OMNI: Bro Bolaji joins an ongoing praise and worship session. Sister Deborah leads the session. The bible study commences. Bro Bolaji dazzles everyone with his deep knowledge of the bible. He quotes the scriptures off hand. Few minutes later the service comes to an end and Bro Bolaji runs after Sister Deborah.

BOLAJI: Excuse me sister. *(Deborah stops).*Truly,
            the mighty unction of the Holy Spirit is
            upon you. You sing like the Cherubim
            and Seraphim, also like the elders before

the throne of God just as it was revealed to John in the book of Revelation. In fact, you are exceptional with an exclusive gift of a unique voice and you use that gift for the praise of Him who reigns over all things. You are beautiful.

DEBORAH: *(Elated)* Thank you sir!

BOLAJI: Sir! For where? I am just a young man Only that I am too old for a boy and too young to be called a man.Just Bolaji will do.

DEBORAH: Okay! Brother Bolaji. Sorry, Bolaji.
BOLAJI: Yes! *(Jumps)* I like it that way. Hope I will see you next Sunday. God bless your week. Sister...?

DEBORAH: Deborah!

BOLAJI: Oh! Deborah. What a name? Debbie!

(They both leave in different directions.)

Scene III
Sister Deborah gets home, prays. Then starts soliloquizing.
DEBORAH: What a good man that Bro Bolaji is. No one has ever complimented my singing like that. He is such a good man. He is also handsome. Maybe God is answering my prayers already. I graduated eight years ago and I have a good job but no man is looking my way. More reason I joined the Choir. Still none of the brothers is forthcoming and those asking me out

are unbelievers. The Pastor says the
Bible warns against being with
unbelievers. Bolly J*(rolls her eyes)* may be
God-sent. Good husbands can only be
found in the church and this is my third
church in my bid to get a man of my own.
God must have sent this one.
(She exits)

Scene IV
(Bro Bolaji in his own home)
BOLAJI: Yepa! See that babe. I was just looking at
her endowment*(draws a figure 8) a*s she
sang. I will follow through. *(exits)*

*OMNI: Weeks run by. Bolaji starts attending weekly
services. They meet during weekly and Sunday services. He is
punctual and joins the workers. He even gets closer to the
pastorate. He sends texts to Deborah day and night. Her
day isn't complete without a message from her Bolly J.*

Scene V
DEBORAH: *(Reads her text)* Hello pretty!*(Smiles)*
Hope you got home with no hassle. I
am highly blessed to have met you.
Do have a restful night. Dream of me.
You are cherished.*(She smiles as she
holds the phone close to her heart.)*
The Lord is answering my prayers.
(She exits)

Scene VI
*OMNI: Meanwhile, the Pastor, having noticed the closeness
between the two, calls Sister Deborah to advise her but she
refuses to heed him, thinking that the Pastor is not interested
in her progress. How can he say a good man like Bolaji could
be deceptive in his presentation? What else could be expected*

*of a man? In her own judgment, he is good and that is that.
The worst, I will quit attending that church. After all, God
is everywhere. Four months later, Deborah is promoted at
work to the post of Assistant Director. And she breaks the
news to Bolaji on the telephone.*

DEBORAH: Guess what? *(Sounding happily)* I have
been promoted to the position of
Assistant Director. I am so happy. I
will be home by 7pm. See you then
(drops the phone). This is God's will!

Scene VII

OMNI:*Bolaji plans the next strategy so well. A man so
cunning in the things of the world.*

BOLAJI: *(Soliloquizing)* Wow! This is a goldmine! I
will just tell her we should have gotten
married by now except that my business is
not doing so fine lately. I know women
so well. She will say that she will sponsor
the wedding. I am clever *(Laughs)*. This is
not my first. I go just dey enjoy on my
own. God don butter my bread be dat. I
need to act fast.

Scene VIII

OMNI: *Just as planned, Bolaji proposed and they got
married two months later in a quiet wedding and they both
stopped attending church, because, according to them, they
don't want any prying eyes. It began as a rosy life together.
Three months later though, she lost her job and that was
when the true color of Bro Bolaji came out. And it certainly
was not color white like the falling snow.*

BOLAJI: I don't even know what I got myself into.

She is so ugly. Fat Pig! She can't even hold
a job. As for me, I can't continue this
kind of life. I better start attending that
big church on the Island as I know I will
meet some classy ladies there. Mehn!
James Bond gats to move on. Actor no
dey die. *(Packs few things and walks out)*

Scene IX

DEBORAH: *(Walks in, crying bitterly!)* He has
absconded o. I never knew Bolly J
could be this heartless. He packed his
things and left. He called me ugly. He
never said that I was too fat when I
was taking care of him, paying his
bills, even when I knew he was lying
that he is having a bad time with his
business when in fact, he has no job.
Mogbe o! What I fear most has
happened o. He is gone o.
      (Cries and goes out.)

END

God works mysteriously. Not long after she dumped all her "How-To" and "How-Not-To" books, she found love. True love.

Johnson was a simple and unassuming guy. They met through a mutual friend and the chemistry was so boiling hot between them. He was the financial comptroller in one of the leading banks. He was advanced in age and had experience in many of life's events. Heartbreaks. Disappointments. Financial crunches.

He was of Ogie extraction.

Johnson wanted to settle down as soon as possible. He proposed six months into their relationship. He was such a very sweet guy. She took him to her parents and vice versa. Both parents were exposed so there never was any discord whatsoever. They just wanted the best for their children. Dacosta stood in for his late father. And after a few months, they got married. Iyabo was now Mrs. Iyabo Segilola Campbell-Oghenero.

Intricately, Johnson had kept his medical condition secret from her. He suffered from leukemia. He was so lively a guy that no one would suspect such an energetic chap covered such a scourge beneath his shirt. Anyway, AIDS NO DEY SHOW FOR FACE was parlance in Nigeria for a reason. They had their honeymoon in Barbados with a stop in London. Their visit to London made it possible for Iyabo to meet her sister in-law for the first time and since Sayo was accompanying them, she met her step mother for the first time, though she was introduced to her as a niece of theirs. Sayo was still in her early teens and could not really decipher what the scenario was. To her, her aunt was her mother and her mother a stranger. And, unbeknownst to her, her Uncle was truly her father.

They are lovely a couple. Grilled in love, Iyabo and Johnson.

WONDERS OF MY HEART

You may go see the worlds
Orient to the Occident;
The temples in China
Niagara, CN towers and the bridge
Connecting Toronto to New York;
Wonders of Canada
Eiffel Tower in Paris,
Buckingham architectural
Ancient civilizations in Egypt.
The Zulus of Southern Africa.
But there is one wonder
You will forever be pleased to see
That is; the beauties
Of my loving heart.

CINDARELLA

Just like a Greek goddess
Extra-ordinary beauty oozing
From inward qualities
A reflecting beam with plaudits
Outwardly obvious
Like mermaid long hair
Curly lips with éclat
Every adoration
Epitome per excellence
A longing,
Delight of everyman
Spell binding voice
Arresting sexes
Till tilting
Great bosom
Tantalizing the beholder
Venus has clicked
The Cupid of a true Romeo
From the maiden sight
Of you.

One would have thought that the love would dwindle after the marriage has been finally contracted. It is such a typical belief of some people in this clime, but this was an exception. Johnson never missed an opportunity to shower love on his spouse at the slightest chance.

Johnson was the first son of his family. His father was a high chief in Ogieland. He was a respected community leader with high cerebral function and knowledge of their culture and tradition. He was a High Chief, indeed.

Two years into their marriage, there had not been a child yet and the pressure was already mounting from Johnson's parents. Johnson was enduring so much heat from his people. He loved his wife very much and was grateful that on many occasions when the issue of their childlessness was raised in the village, she did not accompany him.

"You know what it means if you do not give us a son in good time. You know that I am in my twilight." His old man repeatedly speculated here.

The tradition expected the sitting Oghenero title holder to witness the birth of his grandson in order for the chieftaincy title to remain in their family. Any failure of the stipulations required will amount to the title being transferred to another group. So everyone in the Oghenero Chieftaincy Family was waiting on Johnson to produce. Some were even suggesting getting him another wife. They were waiting. Eagerly!

Johnson remained courageous and always encouraged his wife even in the face of the village heat, despite his failing health, which he never divulged to anyone. He didn't even reveal it to his family members. He had no close friends apart from colleagues at work.

After a long waiting, approximately seven years, Iyabo's womb opened up and she conceived. Before then she underwent series of tests, examinations, observations, and medical trips in and outside of the country. All came to naught.

"Madam, nothing is wrong with you from the medical standpoint of looking at your reproductive organs." The doctors were sure of it. "We can only advise that you take things easy."

She listened and carried out all of their instructions. At one point, she actually gave up going to her shop in order for her to rest and rest adequately. She was always prepared to receive Johnson, anytime, any day, or anywhere. A woman who sought the fruit of the womb would never consider restricting her man access; even when that man seemed tired, she rode him all the same. Her mother and mother in-law had also been bringing various concoctions and herbs considered helpful in making a woman's system tender to her man's semen which might inadvertently yield the desired results. Spiritual cleansing and baths included.

"She must be suffering from astral conjugation." One spiritualist had concluded that. Whatever that meant!

She finally became pregnant after she stopped using any medications, applying concoctions, taking herbs or using spiritual baths.

PREGNANT WOMAN

She lays there
Laughing with pleasure
In a joyous, happy mood
Like someone that
Has eaten the honeycomb
From a beehive.
At three
Tummy protruding
From contagious honey
Colliding with palm kernel
At four
The account becomes fatter
At seven
She walks
Like someone
that has been entombed
With high volume
Of luggage
At nine
Her case becomes
Cyclical
Back the way she started
Trying to ejaculate
The palm kernel she swallowed
With the honey
In great exhaling
And inhaling
With the last unhhh!
Last she laughs
Because of the priceless worth
Of possession
In her possession
Which is now
Hers forever.
Deus wonder.

A boy! A carbon copy of his dad! We will call him Junior. She had suggested that when the scan had informed them that the heartbeat belonged to a boy. But Johnson knew he would not even be the one to name the child as his tradition demanded. He himself was named Johnson Erhiroghene Oghenero by his grandfather, who passed when Johnson was barely seven months old.

The boy had to be taken home. As tradition demanded, he had to be taken home to be initiated into the age long tradition of the Oghenero Chieftaincy rites. At first, Iyabo did not know what that was all about until she got to the village and was made to understand that the infant must be placed in the river and were he to float, he would not be regarded as a bastard but if it were otherwise, the "otherwise" would attest to the simple fact that he was not theirs and that would spell doom for the mother. And, after the first rite, the child must also be left at the riverbank for twenty four hours so as to mingle with the spirits to fortify him for the journey ahead of him. This was done to every male child born into the righteous family of the chief. Woe to a newly born male babe in that family!

It became a big battle. Iyabo refused.

Johnson was compelled by tradition to agree to the rites. He went through the same. So did other men in the family. His refusal would automatically transfer the chieftaincy title to another group. He didn't desire to be the instrument of raising any dysfunction in the family line. Woe, though, to merciless superstitions and traditions!

After many pleas, he assured her that nothing would happen to the child unless he was a bastard, Iyabo bowed. She agreed for the sake of the man, the child, their lineage. And not until the rites were done would such a child be named. The rite also made them confirm the lifespan of the child within the given period.

Common sense should have made one think of what would happen if the child was a true son of his father but dies due to the cold weather he was exposed to at the riverbank? How then would the mother prove her case? But all that was pushed aside in the rush to believe that the truth of the tradition was 'be all and end all' of a ruling male.

True to their fidelity, the child survived. The agony that Iyabo went through all night with her child by the riverbank could only be left to one's imagination. It wasn't pretty, needless to say. Agony is never a sight to joyfully behold. While the other family members went to bed as if nothing was happening, she and Johnson kept a vigil all night with tears of an agonized mother rolling down her cheeks. Johnson assured her that their baby would be fine as long as he had passed the first rite of floating on the water. This other one was for fortification.

Oh the idiocies that are performed in the name of sanctity and tradition!

His grandfather was visibly happy to receive his grandson from the priest the following morning. It was sure indication that the family still possessed the proprietary right to the title. He named him Cornerstone Etanomare Oghenero.

Never mind the mother's wishes.

They returned to their base to continue their life.

A call came through to Iyabo from Johnson's office,

"Madam, you have to rush down to the office clinic!" The doctor had called.

Before she could say anything, the person had dropped the call. Of course, she sensed danger and with that same sense of emergency, she dressed and drove off to Johnson's office.

"We are so sorry, we did our best." The doctor stated this matter of factly, as if they were talking about a contract of sale with some shoes involved.

"But the disease had spread beyond control."

Her husband was officially declared dead then and there. Perfunctorily. Without compassion.

"What disease?" she wailed.

She was stupefied to know that her husband had been suffering from leukemia all the years they had been married. She felt so lost and crushed. Lost because Johnson was gone, and crushed because he had never trusted her enough to share that part of his life with her. Now she was like a woman that was arrested for aiding and abetting her robber husband, who fought violently to exclaim that her husband was never a robber when in actual fact, he was. She hated the ugly truth that men keep secrets and never divulge them no matter the urgency or necessity to share. Secrets, lies, machinations, and superficiality poured down like rain on her head perpetually.

Now the last poem written to her by Johnson made some sense to her:

TO MY HEART

Dearer to my heart
As I go far
Nearer to my mind
As I draw nigh
Priceless to my soul
An invaluable treasure
That you are
For I know
Amor vincit Omnia- Love Conquers all.

The family of Johnson refused to believe even when the Certificate of Death pointed to leukemia as the cause of his death. They held on to the notion that Iyabo must be a witch. How were they to explain that the fortification done on Johnson by the spirits was after all a ruse, because their traditional faith was that no son of theirs would die before the title was passed on to him?

How could he die without succeeding his father, especially when he was the next in line to the title?

A burial rite had to be carried out in the traditional way that an Oghenero title holder must be buried. Being an apparent heir to the title had validated his ascendancy to the seat, so he deserved to be buried as such. Part of the rite was that the wife had to be made to drink some water that was collected from their shrine. If his death was from Iyabo, she would go mad instantly as she drank the water but if not, she would be so graciously allowed her freedom. Iyabo agreed to their terms. And after her vindication, she was free, but only for a few weeks. The battle for the child started. This babe was to take his father's place.

They wanted the custody of the child. The boy, once having survived the brutal initiation on shortly after birth, had no other fate but to become a chieftain. And that would be soon as the sitting Oghenero was in his twilight. The near newborn would have to be close to him so as to learn the rites; those age old rites. In fact, they desired him to grow on the old man's lap, going through tutelage for the traditional ascendancy to the title.

"He is just nine months old!" Iyabo retorted!

Battle Royale.

Dacosta had to come into town to secure the service of a lawyer for his sister as the battle raged on. They would have to use an attorney in order to determine where tradition stopped in a modern society. It would be insane for a child to be separated from his mother at such a very tender age. Though Johnson's family was ready to let her have all the appurtenances but equally, they were ready to do anything to obtain custody of the child. In this entire imbroglio, little Etanomare, Quokka-like was bubbly with life. No one should have doubted the paternity of the child. He was a replica of his father. Lively. And strong. For who but the strong could have survived what he had already in his incredibly young life?!

"It is purely inhuman and irrational to human dignity for an infant to be separated from its mother based on the idea of fulfilling cultural or traditional demands." Barrister Ayegbogbon Rorase had submitted his opinion. He was a leading voice in advocating for Child Rights .

"Don't let us belabor ourselves with legal verbosity and technicalities, since the law itself is meant to be adjudicated reasonably. The baby needs his mother to grow into a mentally, physically, and socially fit individual. That is the core tenet here. A mother is fundamental!"

One would wonder where these lawyers learned their words from. But in the real sense, language, especially the English language, is the premise of communication in this profession. Law must denote its seriousness and grandeur via a lexicon that is commanding and eloquent simultaneously. To be otherwise, the Law might be taken too lightly.

The defendant's lawyer, Kodjo Onakpoma, a renowned Senior Advocate of great repute was hired by the Oghenero Chieftaincy Family.

The ties of the professionals on all sides were coincidental and rather dramatic. Both attorneys, defence and opposing, were close friends of Dacosta. They were also classmates in Eko Boys High School, Lagos. And, strangely enough, the sitting judge was an old student of Eko Boys as well.

Kodjo argued his case in the roundabout style of the legal profession.

Litigation is very interesting, especially when you meet lawyers who can argue from angles that are unusual to the common mind but actually are logical.

He submitted that, as much as Etanomare needed his mother, he also needed a father figure. Since his father was deceased, the onus passed to the paternal family of the child. And they were ever ready and happy to take over. Being a reputable and respected family of record, the family wanted the child and mother to be in their care. That care would see to it that both would be adequately catered to. And, even if the mother liked, she could marry from amongst their clan. Further, she could go outside of their clan to marry according to her own choice and freewill. Their major interest was the boy.

The judge, understanding the sensitivity of the case, tradition and reason, adjourned the case for further hearing, with the child left in the custody of the mother, pending the determination of the case. It was a clash of many interests. Tradition. Reason. Ethnicities. Alma Mater. Confraternity.

At one of their night outings, Kodjo, in company with the judge and Dacosta, discussed the issue at hand. It was dubious practice, but done nonetheless.

"'How do you think this issue should be resolved?" The judge asked this of the others.

Dacosta, a man of culture and tradition himself, knew the family was just concerned about receiving the child in order to ensure their continued possession of the title. That title had been in their family for over seventy years, and losing it might mean another long wait for such an offer to return to their family. Hence, they would do anything necessary to legally possess this child. He also knew that his sister might never give birth to another child again as she had entered into menopause and the only thing that would give her joy would be to have the child exclusively in her care.

The brother, Dacosta, was ready to do anything for his sister. He would do anything within the confines of reasonable sense to make her happy. Moreover, he was keeping to his promise to make the only sibling he had left happy at all times.

The judge looked at both men and said, "I shouldn't divulge this to you but to tell you guys the truth, I am torn in all of this."

Truly, the denial of either is unfair. How can one rule in this kind of a situation? But one can and one must!

They looked forlorn.

It was either that the law was inadequate or that the law was determined to save face. Indefinite adjournment, *sine die*, was what was applied; not officially, but actually. That was the ploy used by this judge in his court for this case, indefinite postponement. The lack of courage and responsibility was huge. The court should have been ashamed. But, this judge just moved on. That was easiest for him.

"The mother will continue to have custody of the child till further determination." That was the judge's ruling. At least he fell on the side of humanity and mercy. The tradition already spoke for their egregious self-centeredness, superstitions, and mandates that tortured even the newborn. Naturally, one should not expect otherwise. For goodness sake, *ceteri paribus*. The mother had the breasts and milk of life, and so, of course, the child went to the mother.

It was unofficially and permanently adjudicated. Rare that a tradition, no matter its implausibility, did not win out.

Sayo would not leave Dedapo for anything in the world. She vowed to stay with her marital obligations come rain, come shine, till death do them part.

Dedapo proposed as soon as they got home from the clinic that day where Sayo was rushed to after her exhaustion. But the medical team confirmed she was a few weeks in. Pregnant, for sure!

Dedapo was so happy. He could not hold his joy. So he proposed that it was high time they took their relationship to the next level. But one might wonder what was to be taken to the next level. They had lived together as man and wife, unofficially, for years.

It was a society wedding. People flew in from all over. Traditionally, it was expected that a background check would be done on the couple. But who would blame anyone in this case as they were already married at common law and such formalities would naturally be ignored.

Dacosta had relied on the submissions of his friends back home, most of whom were busy professionals or businessmen cum politicians. They had only asked Sayo to bring her fiancé to them and after a few quick questions asked, they believed that he was a great guy because Dedapo, always at his best when performing, usually dazzled anyone with his brilliance and education. They forgot to check his character, though. What makes a man is his character. Nothing else! Seeing the nut, they overlooked the kernel.

The crème-de-la-crème of the society, aristocrats, professionals, politicians, businessmen and plenipotentiaries, all had come to grace this occasion of one of their own. Eventually, it was payback time. Dacosta had been helpful and had graced many of their occasions in the past. One might have thought that he lived in Nigeria as he came home regularly, keeping in touch with his roots. He would fly in from wherever he was, to honor them during their celebrations; even the miniscule of those frequent occasions.

Dacosta jumped at any opportunity to leave home because he was finding his Rwandan wife too boring and old for his liking. He knew well that she would not come with him to Africa so he would tell her he was visiting Nigeria to attend a party, deliberately leaving out the fact of enjoying the party, but more so enjoying the retinue of fresh flesh paraded before him. How kind of him. He was one of the Big Men at Lagos parties and so nubile young women were lined up for him, each and every time. He was cognizant that Nigerian hospitality included this array of treats for the virile man. Call them what you will, these consorts knew how to have fun. And that was exactly what he came there for!

The officiating Reverend was the antithesis of some sorts. He had preached that, "a man will leave his mother and father to cleave unto his wife and they both will be one flesh."

That was the popular Genesis Two, Twenty Fourth sermon for a normal wedding ceremony. But his records showed that he is currently facing a divorce proceedings from his third marriage.

He is a good friend of the President. He denied his political interests even though the blindest of the blind knew otherwise. Some even referred to him as the spiritual lord of the President. His wife had caught him pants down many times with other women, married and single, in the name of deliverance, prayer, and counseling, hence, his lack of success at marriage. His current spouse was seeking a divorce as fast as possible.

"I wonder how some women can be so daft?" This critic continued by saying, "How can someone tell you to go nude in order to be delivered from spiritual attack!"

The ludicrous notion of that thought was: how can one explain the role of a man of God who is at the center of a free-for-all fight by some women who are laying proprietary claim to his love?

"He is mine!" This one of his women had shouted.

"I brought you to this church for deliverance and now you are sleeping with him!" Another of his worshippers had bellowed.

None of these women is his wife. Then what should the wife do if they own his love? Yes, she was doing exactly that; seeking divorce.

Even so, many people trooped to his church for his self-acclaimed vast knowledge of the Bible and his grandiloquence in teaching the word of God. He was a powerful dresser, always dangling a necklace of outlandish amounts of gold karats made into a crucifix reaching his torso. That adornment might have sat well with a rappa' too. Lately, some youth called him, Jigga.

A crucifix around his and many other necks had become objects of mere adornment, not remotely an insignia of piety anymore.

Anyway, the couple was admonished to be steadfast in love, and true to one another just as Adam and Eve, who were naked in the Garden of Eden and were not ashamed of one another. This was a message coming from a Reverend who also was the head of the cult of the Knights. An oxymoron perhaps?!

The couple returned home that night. Tired from the day's activities, they laughed as they relived the message from the pulpit. Lord Reverend indeed!

Sayo looked Dedapo in the eyes again and repeated the vows:

COME WHAT MAY, I WILL STICK
WITH YOU

That is a woman for you. She gives you everything.

Iyabo played her many parts in the wedding ceremony. The mother. The hostess. The hospitality manager. But deep down within her she believed that the marriage would crash as she saw Dedapo as an irresponsible man out to take advantage of her niece. She didn't believe otherwise as her wisdom was based on experience.

Since the demise of Johnson, while the battle for the custody of Etanomare raged on for many years, Iyabo tried her hands at many relationships, always hoping that she might achieve some solace in the protection that a man's arms would offer her. But, in all, she ended up with heartbreak at each trial. Where was logic? Logic would assume that multiple failures might indicate the need for new ways. Logic, though, was not emotion.

One of her relationships ended in a fracas between the man's legal wife and her. The man had told her he was a widower and that his two kids were taken to the village to be with his mother and he was unwilling to put up with a child anymore. Their opinions coincided as she was not willing to have another child either. They had so much fun the little time that they shared together, until the man's wife showed up. She had been living in the village with her own mother and their six children. This father, this reprobate, came home every two weeks but he had not come these past three months. The wife was fortunate to have overheard a comment that hinted that a certain woman had snatched her man. She saw it herself in his growing absence. It became a big mess as the woman made a scene , tore Iyabo's blouse, and shouted for her to leave her man alone. So disgraceful.

Another one involved a younger man who was about university age and whose parents had to come burgle him out of Iyabo's house. She was repeatedly warned never to come near their son again. A cougar, a cradle robber as she was abusively called.

So many relationship messes in order to have her own man.

God wondered if they were worth it.

She decided to visit some marabouts for spiritual consultations as some friends had told her that she must be suffering from the spirit of Johnson still hovering about her and that made it difficult for her to remarry.

In one of her deliverance sessions, a marabout told her that he would have to go inside her to eliminate the deposits that Johnson had left which kept her from being totally free.

She feigned ignorance as she asked, "How?"

"Like a man and a woman." The marabout smiled as he rubbed her back.

She rose up, left and never went back there again. Nor did she visit any other place to seek spiritual cleansings or deliverance. She got home and burst into tears. She had been used and duped. Again! She recalled her many spiritual baths where she had to be bathed by the marabout in the river. She felt humiliated.

Desperation can lead anyone to fall for anything. Iyabo wept for herself and her plight.

But the humiliation went deep enough this time to make her realize something, something powerful about herself. It made her realize that she did not need a man to be complete. That her happiness and joy were inward and all that she needed to do was to go deep inside herself, seeking, truly inside where her core lay.

It was time for her to draw from those strengths and succeed where no man has ever led her: to succeed independently, on her own.

Thank goodness she is blessed with a son.

She was blessed by so much.

THY HOLINESS

Blur vividness
Momentum for insuperable
Clamorous sleuthing
A running lame
A hearing deaf
A crystal clear speaking dumb
With no babbling
"Alleludoubt"
One rushes to the dome
Looking for the conjurer
Am I to get a passport
Marrying a visa
Before I get to the cherished abode!
Where today
Will I get a true surgeon?

SOCIETAL FRAGMENTS

Glossary

Omo aijoberi- a depraved individual.(Yoruba Language.)

Opa eyin- Herbal drink; an aphrodisiac.

Jeje- Easy. (In the Yoruba language.)

Awuf- Freebies. (In Pidgin English.)

Wey- That. (In Pidgin English.)

Sey na- Is it? (In Pidgin English.)

Baba dudu- A dark skinned man but is used connotatively to mean ale. (In the Yoruba language.)

Two Face Idibia (2Face)- is a stage name of a prominent Nigerian singer but because of the way the name sounds it is connotatively used to mean a woman's two breasts and her backside.

Mogbe- An exclamatory remark that signals doom. (In the Yoruba language.)

Badooo- Coded name for a bad person.

Abeg- Please.

Adebutu Kessington- He is the founder of a foremost lotto company in Nigeria.

Ijebu man- A man from one of the tribes of the Yoruba people of South West Nigeria. They are believed to be economical in their fiscal dealings. (In the Yoruba language.)

Baba ose oku itoju mi- A song that says, "Thank you Lord for your provision."

Cheddah- A coded name for money

Enta- Enter.

Gbese- Debt(In the Yoruba language.)

Wetin- What.

Mogbe morogo- I am doomed. (In the Yoruba language.)

Oju kokoro- Greed. (In the Yoruba language.)

Ololufe mi- My love. (In the Yoruba language.)

Isiwo- A town in Ogun state, South West, Nigeria.

(A(De)Dara- Worthy of praise. (In the Yoruba language.)

(A)De)Dapo- Royal confluence. (In the Yoruba language.)

Jaiyesimi- Let the world rest; used usually for a still birth.(In the Yoruba language.)

(A)De)Sayo- A beautiful daughter. (In the Yoruba language.)

Iretiola- Hope. (In the Yoruba language.)

Oladepo-Wealth has come to its place(Yoruba)

Olowogbowo- A location in Lagos, South West Nigeria.

Igbayilola- Now is the time of wealth. (In the Yoruba language).

Iyabo(de)- A mother has come; usually given to the first girl begotten after the demise of a matriarch of the family. (In the Yoruba language.)

(Segi)lola- Ornaments are wealth. (In the Yoruba language.)

(Ola)Dehinde- Wealth has returned. (In the Yoruba language.)

Oluwanisola- God gives wealth. (In the Yoruba language.)

Aduke- Sweet to pamper. (In the Yoruba language.)

(A)Bodunde- One who walks in with the festival.

Isale Eko- A location in Lagos, South West Nigeria.

Yanga- Hard to get. (In Pidgin English.)

(A)Bolaji- A rise with wealth.

Yepa- Exclamation of shock.

Actor no dey die- A hero never gives up.

(Oghe)nero- There is God. (In the Ogie dialect.)

(Erhi)r(oghene)- The spirit of God. (In the Ogie dialect.)

(E)ta)nomare-   Freed from blame. (In the Ogie dialect.)

Ayegbogbon – Life is full of intrigues.

Rorase- Tread gently.

Kodjo-   Born on Monday. (In the language of Ghana.)

Onakpoma- Who creates life.

dibia- A seer.

Menticide- Derangement to the point of suicide by bomb.

Parole: A slang that means underground moves.

SOCIETAL FRAGMENTS